Don't Let Them In

Six Tales of Terror

Elizabeth Fields

CONTENTS

"The road to our dreams is often paved with nightmares."

-Elizabeth Fields

THE DEBT COLLECTOR

The branches whip my face as I run further and deeper into the dark woods. I know my leg is bleeding, and with each lunge, I become more aware of the blinding pain. No matter how much it hurts, I have to keep my pace. My lungs feel heavy, and my head is pounding, but I have no choice but to keep running. My entire body is becoming numb, but I dare not stop. I dare not look back either. I know it's behind me; I can feel it on my heels. As long as I'm still running, I'm still alive. I could tell you what is chasing me, but you wouldn't believe me. Maybe if I told you why I'm being hunted, you would understand.

The nightmare began about five years ago. Correction, it would be exactly five years ago, to this very day. Some would call it a dream come true, but I'm standing by nightmare. That's when I met *her*. I was a down and out actor, who couldn't catch a break. I thought I'd finally fallen into some luck when I was cast in a pilot for a sitcom on a major network. I was on top of the world the whole week of filming. I just knew this was it. This was my big break, but then, the ax fell. We got word that the network backed out, and production had been canceled. To make matters worse, my agent dumped me, claiming I was bad mojo; whatever the hell that means. This also meant I would soon be broke again and back to ground zero. Sure, I got paid for the pilot, but after rent and the six grand in credit card debt I'd just paid off, I was dry. It's also not as if people were lined up to give me a shot. I wasn't the best looking guy. I was tall and skinny and had awkward features. I was what people in the biz call a "character actor", which makes things a little more difficult since you have to wait around for the chance to audition for parts that only require someone of your particular uniqueness. Hollywood isn't exactly bending over backwards to include the unique or beauty challenged these days. And so, on that night, October 16th, I found myself drowning my sorrows in some shit hole of a dive bar in the valley.

I sat at the bar, a half empty glass of whiskey over ice in front of me. It was my fourth. I sat and watched it for about twenty minutes. At first I was thinking about how horrible I felt, but then I became hypnotized by the glass and stopped thinking all together. I watched blankly as the drops of condensation released from their spots on the glass and rolled swiftly down to the bar napkin below. I almost didn't look up when she came in. I wish now that I hadn't, but something tells me that even if I hadn't noticed her, she would have found me.

I heard the door open faintly in the background and felt a soft breeze come toward me as the large door shut. The air outside wafted in, smelling of cigarettes and different colognes and perfumes, a scent that seemed a confusing mixture of a fun night out and desperation. Out of the corner of my eye, there was a beautiful, glowing red; my attention was quickly turned in that direction. There she was, the most beautiful woman I had ever seen in real life, maybe the most beautiful woman ever. Her skin looked as if it were delicately carved from ivory. Every feature on her face was perfection. Her eyes flashed a deep green, and her lips, painted so perfectly, reminded me of a ripe strawberry. Her red dress hugged her flawless curves as she floated toward me at the bar. She looked as if she were traveling on air in slow motion. I couldn't have been the only one to notice this creature, but I couldn't look away, not even for a second, to see the reaction I knew she was getting. All eyes had to be on her, and mine weren't able to glance away. She took the seat next to mine and held up her right index finger to signal the bartender. He eagerly made his way to her, leaving another order incomplete. She whispered her drink of choice in his ear, and he, as if in a trance, fulfilled her request with a quickness, and upon returning, he noted that her drink was on the house.

She graciously accepted the gift and took a sip from the straw as he looked on longingly. She thanked him again, informing him in her angelic voice that this drink would be all for now, and he turned reluctantly back to his other patrons.

As she took another drink, I finally realized that I had been staring at her the entire time, and I decided to pry my eyes away from her. She had to be tired of all the attention, all the men in the bar ogling her. She seemed so sweet, so delicate.

I returned my gaze to my own drink. Most of the sweat from the outside of the glass had already fallen. My ice was nearly melted. I picked up the glass, and in one swift motion, downed the rest of my malt.

"Rough day?" The soft, serene voice was pointed in my direction. I was terrified that I would say something stupid, but what the hell, the day couldn't possibly get any worse, so I thought, *hey, why not talk to this girl?*

"Yeah, you could say that," I replied in my sad attempt to sound cool and indifferent.

"I'm sorry to hear that," she said, sounding genuinely concerned. I was surprised. I was even more surprised that she chose to continue the conversation. "I haven't had the best day myself," she continued, "but you know, tomorrow is a new day. You could wake up and find everything has changed... even for the better."

"Ah, so you're an optimist? Don't meet many of those out here." I knew I was sounding lame, but I really didn't know what to say to such a pretty face.

"Well, maybe you're not hanging out with the right people." She flashed a smile at me. I was confused. This woman was flirting with me. My next thought was that I was either completely misinterpreting the situation, or this gorgeous woman was some kind of escort, who probably meant to go to a much more upscale establishment but ended up in this dive by mistake. I kept the conversation up anyway.

"Maybe," I said as I turned and extended my hand. "I'm Greg."

"They call me Alex." She held my hand a few seconds longer than the usual handshake. Her skin felt like velvet.

"Who would *they* be?"

"Oh, you know, people, acquaintances, friends, I suppose." She smiled playfully to the side and swept her hair behind her ear with her now free right hand. "Maybe we could be friends." She was now touching my hand again, but this wasn't a handshake, this was flirting. I revisited my previous theory that Alex might be in the business of pleasure for money. Money I didn't have, and though she was the most elegant woman I'd ever met, I would never consider paying for a girl.

"I'm sorry. Please, don't take this the wrong way, but what exactly is your line of work?" I could have probably asked with a little more ease, but this was how it came out. I eagerly awaited her response.

"I'm sort of in public relations," she cooed. She wouldn't break eye contact, so I had to.

"Yeah, I thought so. Look, Alex, I don't think I'm what you're looking for tonight. I don't really go in for that sort of thing."

"What thing? Oh..." She laughed. "I'm not a hooker, Greg. I help people get what they want, but I'm not a hooker."

"Oh, I'm so sorry. I just assumed..." This was coming out badly. "I mean, not that you, I just mean, well, girls that look like you, who are, you know, phenomenal, don't usually converse with guys like me in bars."

"Hmm. We'll just say that was a compliment and leave it at that." She took her hand away for a moment to pick up her glass and finish her drink. She motioned to the bartender for another round for the both of us.

"I'm sorry; I didn't mean to..."

"It's alright, Greg. So tell me, what would you want most in the world right now?"

"Really? What are you? Some kind of genie?"

4

"Let's say I am. What could I do for you?"

"Well," I said as I entertained the thought, "I guess I would wish for another shot at acting."

"Ah, I could do that," she replied while the bartender set down our fresh glasses.

"Oh here, let me." I went for my deflated wallet.

"No, no. This one's on me," she said sweetly. I thought that was exceptionally nice of her, though thinking about it now, she never did pay for those drinks. The bartender just walked away and never asked her to pay for a thing.

"Thank you." I tipped my glass toward her to toast. "To new friends!"

"To new friends," she repeated. She sipped from the top of the sugar rimmed drink and carefully placed it back onto its napkin.

"Where were we..." she continued, "ah, yes, your career. What do you think would make you happy?"

"Well, I guess since we're just dreaming here, I would say, I want it all. I want to be a mega movie star with the house in the hills, the beautiful girl on my arm, and all the accessories, you know, cars, boats, villas in whatever country I feel like visiting, and total access to every and any event I want."

"Say I could do that for you, what would you give me in return?"

"I would give my left arm for all that." I laughed and took another drink. "Then again, if I only had one arm that would kind of be a bummer."

"What if you had five years? Five years that could be everything you ever wanted and more. You could have five years to live the life you want and love every minute of it, then what?"

"Five is kind of a small number, isn't it?"

"Maybe to some, but it would be five years, jam packed with realized dreams. You could have anything and everything you've always wanted."

"Well, what happens after the five years are up?"

"Does it really matter?" She smiled slyly again.

"No, I guess not, not if all my dreams would come true. Better to live a wonderful five years and kick the bucket having had and done everything I ever wanted than to live the rest of my life miserable."

"You mean that?" She looked a little serious for the kind of hypothetical conversation I thought we were having, but I didn't notice the glimmer then, the glow in her eye.

"Sure I mean it! I would sign that deal in a heartbeat!" I laughed and drank some more. I was definitely feeling the warmth of the liquor.

"So you say you would give your life, but what about your soul?"

"Well, sure. Why not?" I laughed again and looked at her as I swigged the rest of my whiskey.

"Alright then. Done. I will give you five years. Five of the most wonderful years you could ever imagine, full of success, love, and admiration, and when those years are up, you owe me. I get your soul." She smiled as she took her last drink. She then took her hand and placed it on my leg.

"Well it sounds like I'm making a deal with the devil." I smiled as I felt my head begin to swim with the happy effects of just enough alcohol.

"Something like that. So do we have a deal?"

"Sure we do! What the hell, right?" I was now signaling the bartender for more.

Three drinks later I found myself back at my North Hollywood apartment with my new friend. The rest of that night is a blur, but I do know it was one of the best nights of my life, and I certainly didn't have to pay for it, or so I thought.

I woke up the following morning to the tune of the *Bonanza* theme. My cell phone was ringing. I took a second before reaching for it to look around with my fuzzy, tired eyes. To my left was Alex; she was really there; I hadn't just dreamt her up. I grabbed my cell phone and saw the name "Stanley Hodge" on the screen. It was my agent, or my ex-agent rather.

I didn't want to answer. I didn't want to listen to him tell me again what a giant nothing I was, but out of morbid curiosity I clicked the answer button.

"Hello?" I sounded like a frog.

"Greg, buddy. It's your pal, Stanley. How are you doing?"

"Uh... fine..." I found it difficult to mask my confusion.

"Look, the other day I said some things, and well, you know, I'm just under a ton of pressure here, so I hope you didn't take me seriously. Anyway, guess who is top pick for the lead in the next Dorian Chase film?"

"Uh... I couldn't tell you..." I was still confused.

"You, buddy! You! All the way. I just got the call. You're in! You're a star, baby! We're in negotiations right now, but it's basically a done deal. I'll call you when we've finalized pay rates, and you can come in and sign contracts."

"Wait... what?" I asked. Was this a joke? My confusion was still there, but I could feel my entire body heating up with excitement. I was suddenly very aware of where my stomach was. It felt like it was full of rocks.

"You're it, Greg! You're the man! Okay, I have to get back to this, but I will be calling you, buddy. Congratulations, superstar!"

I heard a click in my ear; Stanley was gone. I stared at my phone for what felt like an eternity trying to replay everything I just heard. It slowly began to saturate, and then it clicked. I was it! I was the man! I jumped out of bed and started dancing around the room. My head was swirling, mostly from the previous night of drinking, but I didn't care; I just kept dancing like an idiot.

Alex woke slowly and turned toward me, watching me do some weird combination of the sprinkler and the running man.

"Wow," she said. "Somebody is having a good morning."

"Yes! Somebody is! Me! For once! It's me!" I leapt toward her and gave her a giant kiss. "You're my good luck charm. That's it. You can't ever leave." I laughed and jumped back up.

So it began, my climb, or rather rocket, straight to the top. I was on fire, booking jobs left and right. I was constantly filming, going to Hollywood parties, being photographed everywhere I went, and being rushed by star struck fans. It was everything I'd ever dreamed and more. I was making huge salaries and living the life of luxury. I had it made with cars, a house in the hills, an apartment in New York, vacations in exotic locations, and a beautiful woman on my arm. Alex was there by my side through it all. She was amazing. We never discussed marriage or doing the family thing. I was so caught up in my career, I never really thought about it. I guess in the back of my head, I just figured we'd settle down when I'd had my fill of the spotlight, or it had had its fill of me, but it never dimmed. I was on top year after year. I actually had to turn things down I was so busy. Who would have ever thought, me, Greg the nerd from Nowhere, Oklahoma, so famous and in demand that I get to turn things down?

Five years went by in a flash. I had hit after hit in the box office. I was the most sought after celebrity in the world with hundreds of magazine covers and a handful of awards to prove it.

That brings us to tonight. Alex and I had just attended the premiere of my latest film, a film in which I had played the lead in a romantic comedy. My agent wasn't so sure about me doing a romantic comedy after all the action and drama films I had completed over the years, but I was really excited about it, and as it turns out, he was fine with the idea once he saw the incredible amount of money they were offering me. His percentage bought him a new luxury car and a large down payment on a vacation home in The Hamptons.

Alex and I decided to skip the party, so we could have our own celebration. She offered to drive, so I could relax and revel in the high of adoration some more. I loved premieres. Everyone was always so happy and doting, usually doting over me, something I never tired of.

I was too busy recalling the nights events to realize how long we'd been driving. We were on the highway quite some time before I even realized we were already past Oxnard.

"Where are we going?" I questioned. I was sure my loving girlfriend had cooked up some sort of amazing surprise for me.

"Shh…" she replied melodically, "you'll ruin it. It'll be a while longer though. Why don't you just close your eyes, and we'll be there before you know it."

So I did. I closed my eyes and drifted off to sleep. I'm not sure how long we were driving, but I woke some time later to the engine cutting off. I adjusted myself in the leather seat, stretching and yawning. I looked to my left to see Alex's lovely face, but she had a strange expression. It was stoic. I'd never seen this face before. I'd always seen her in only three ways, happy, sexy, and calm, never anything else. Come to think of it, I had never seen her sad or angry or even slightly disappointed. I began searching my brain for conflict. Could it be Alex and I had really never had an argument? I realized we hadn't. I had no memory of us ever fighting, or of us even having a bad day. Actually, I couldn't remember the last time I'd had a bad day since we met. It was odd I hadn't realized this until now, but then again, when you're happy, you're happy. Why would you think about that?

"Where are we?" I looked around and saw a faintly moonlit dirt road stretched out in front of us and dark trees to either side. She didn't respond, so I continued, "everything alright?"

"Let's go for a walk," she said plainly. She opened the driver's side door and stepped out into the night.

"Alright." I joined her at the edge of the trees. We appeared to be in a forest of some kind. I had no idea where we were or how long we had been driving, but we had clearly gone a lot farther than Ventura County.

She softly grabbed my hand, as she had done many times before, and led me into the trees. Alex was wearing a formal dress and heels, yet she seemed not at all phased by the uneven terrain. She walked effortlessly and elegantly as if she were floating. I'd always loved watching her move.

"Where are we going?" I asked, beginning to get a little concerned. This seemed so unusual.

"All will be revealed," she replied.

All will be revealed? It danced around in my head. She sounded like a reality show host. I chuckled nervously.

We walked for about ten minutes, guided by the moonlight. Neither of us had a flashlight, but Alex looked as if she knew exactly where she was going, so I just went with it. She finally stopped at a small clearing. I stood next to her, trying to understand what we were doing as I searched the trees around us. I wasn't very comfortable being surrounded by these woods. They suddenly seemed so much darker and completely uninviting. A chill fell over us, and my discomfort was heightened.

"Alex, maybe we should head back to the car," I suggested. She was wearing a strapless gown, and I didn't have my jacket to lend her. It was back in the car.

"No, no," she replied, "this is our destination."

"Really? Here? What exactly are we going to do out here?"

"Well, first I need to ask you a couple questions." She turned toward me, her beautiful face glowing as the moon lit her skin. "Would you say your dreams have come true?"

"Yes, of course I would." I took her hands into mine to reassure her. We'd never discussed our future; I was sure this was the purpose of our little excursion. She wanted to have the marriage talk.

"Would you say that the last five years have been the best years of your life, and you've had everything you've ever wanted?"

"Yes, Alex," I replied as I leaned in for a kiss.

She stopped me, putting her right index finger to my lips.

"I'm glad you've had the life you've always dreamed of. I'm glad that I could help you get what you've always wanted." There was that emotionless face again. She had a blank expression, which made my stomach knot up. I started to fear she was about to end our relationship.

"Alex, you know I love you..."

"That's beautiful, Greg. I'm just happy that you've had a good life."

"And it's going to continue," I cut in, "we're going to be very happy."

"Well, you've been happy, and now, I can be happy too. I held up my end of the bargain, and now I have to ask you to hold up yours."

"What? What bargain? I'm sorry, Alex, you've lost me." I searched her eyes for clues. I was sure that I was about to get an ultimatum. Marry her or else. Just because we never discussed it, didn't mean she didn't want it.

"Five years ago, this very night, we met in that bar. We met, and we made a deal."

"A deal? I'm sorry..." I chuckled to myself as I tried to recall that night. It was pretty much a blur. All I really remembered was that it was the beginning of the rest of my new life.

"Yes, a deal. I said I would give you everything you ever wanted in this world, and in return, you offered yourself. Tonight, I intend to collect on that debt."

"Oh," I laughed as it came back to me. "I remember. Right, right, my deal with the devil. Alex, honey, you're too much. Look, why don't we go back to the car and find a nice hotel somewhere and talk. It's freezing out here."

"Sorry, dear, we can't do that. My boss would really like to see a return on his investment. I really need to handle this business now. So you can just go ahead and surrender your soul, or I can take it. I recommend the first option. The whole taking thing can get really messy and, well, painful."

"Okay, Alex." I laughed, but something in her eyes told me she was serious. "Alright, so I'm supposed to believe you're what? Satan?"

"Oh, no. Thank you, but no. I do some work for the man downstairs, but I'm just a negotiator. I make the deals and then collect the payments. A debt collector, that's what I am. Don't act so surprised. Did you really think a woman this perfect would hang around someone like you? Did you really think that you were such a hot commodity, the movie industry couldn't live without you? Who really gets that lucky?"

"Okay, you're serious aren't you? Did you take something at the premiere tonight?" I said jokingly, but I was honestly concerned. "Are you feeling alright? Come on, let's get you back to the car." I held my hand out for her to take. She met my hand with hers but didn't step with me. Her grip tightened, and I turned back toward her, confused. As I looked at her, her grip got even tighter, and then, I felt a sudden burst go through my hand and through my body. The last five years I'd experienced flashed through my head at warp speed. The film sets, the flashing bulbs of the paparazzi, the autographs, the white sand beaches, the parties, the martinis, the money, all came back to me at the same time.

The last memory flashed, and the energy left my body. I quickly withdrew my hand and leapt backward toward the trees behind me.

"What the hell are you? What was that?" I asked as I trembled with fear.

"I already told you, Greg. I think you know what I am, and you know what I've done for you. Apparently, you needed that little reminder. You're being a little ungrateful. Don't worry; you're not the only one to freak out once the bill comes due. This is perfectly natural, but I *will* get payment. It's up to you how I get it, but I will get it." Her eyes glowed; a red flicker took over her pupils.

"Oh, God."

"No, Greg, He can't really help you now. He turned his back on you the day you turned your back on Him."

"I never..."

"Yes, you did. You chose this life for yourself. You traded your soul for a mere five years of indulgence. They kind of frown upon that sort of thing up there."

"This... this isn't what I meant. No, I don't believe you," I didn't dare take my eyes off hers. They were lit up like a fireplace. I didn't know what she was capable of.

"Believe it. Think Greg. Have you ever experienced sadness, poverty, despair, or even illness in the last five years? When was the last time you had the flu, Greg? When was the last time you had to worry about anything other than having a good time?"

"I..." I couldn't remember. She was right. I hadn't had the flu or a cold in years. I hadn't felt stress or discontent in such a long time, I didn't even remember what it felt like. Even fear was something I had forgotten all about until this very moment. All I had known the last five years was happiness and utter joy. I was living the dream, and perfect as it was, I couldn't remember ever taking the time to appreciate it. My life was good, and I sort of just expected it to continue on that way. Obviously, it wasn't going to.

"That's right. You've had everything. You took it all for granted. Don't feel bad; most of them make the same mistake. They never really know what they have until the expiration date. If it makes you feel any better, you're one of my favorites."

"Five years, Alex, five years we spent together." I was still searching for some reason, something to make sense of this situation I was now in.

"Five years for a mortal is like five minutes to us. It's a really small price to pay to get you on our team. Enough chit chat, lover. Let's get to it. There's just the tiny little matter of your soul we need to discuss."

"No, I won't let you," I declared.

"Too bad you feel that way. It could have gone so much more smoothly for you. We're just going to have to take it then."

We're? She said "we're". My body went numb with terror. She raised her hands up, closed her eyes, and whispered something I couldn't understand. Her hands grew; they nearly doubled in size. Her manicure suddenly changed into hideous claws. Her eyes glowed more intensely than before as she settled her gaze back on me. That's when I heard it. From deep in the woods behind her, I heard a snarling. I had no idea what was coming, but I knew it was coming fast. I turned to run, and she caught my leg with her razor sharp claws. My flesh ripped as she dug into my leg. The frozen feeling I had just a moment before was suddenly replaced with searing pain. I managed to free myself, and Alex laughed as I ran from her.

She didn't follow me.

And so, here I am, running. As I dodge branches and jump over brush, her laugh becomes more and more faint, but the snarling grows closer. Whatever it was she conjured up to sic on me is gaining. I know it's close. It's almost right on top of me. I'm far to scared to turn and face whatever it is. I can feel its hot breath on me, and I can smell its foul odor. The dog-like growling is almost in my ear as it thuds close behind. I know this creature is much larger than me. I don't stand a chance. I know once I stop running, it's over. So I will keep running, ignoring the pain in my leg. I will keep running until I pass out or until it catches me. All I can think about is what I should have done. I should have gone back to Oklahoma and joined my dad's business. I should have learned to be happy with being ordinary. At least I'd still have a soul... and I definitely wouldn't be here in these woods. I guess if something is too good to be true, don't offer to buy it a drink; even if no one picks up the bar tab, you'll end up paying for it more than you know.

PLENTY OF FLESH IN THE SEA

I was eight years old the first time I tasted the blood of another person. It was my brother's. Sam and I were always close. He was a year older and very protective of me, his only sister. Since the beginning, we were a team. We were all we had. Our mother was an alcoholic and heroin addict, dependent on whatever scumbag would help her get her fix. She didn't give a shit what happened to us as long as she was taken care of. She'd let them do whatever they wanted. *They* being the many nameless, faceless large figures that would beat us, or worse, completely forget about us. We lived in a dilapidated, two story house, the only thing our father left behind. He worked in a factory, and according to our mother, he died in a freak accident involving a very large machine and faulty wiring. The way she told it, messed up as she was all the time, we never got the whole story, but we always imagined he was electrocuted by one of the machines he was working with.

Back to the day I first realized my love for human blood. I'll never forget that day. It was a Saturday. I know it was a Saturday because Sam and I were trying to sneak a cartoon in before our mother and her boyfriend of the week got home that morning from one of their binges. We weren't allowed to watch TV. Hell, we weren't really even allowed to be downstairs. We were supposed to stay out of sight; that way Mom could get away with the illusion that she didn't have any kids, for a while at least, but they always found out about us, which sometimes made them leave and other times gave them two little people to take their anger out on.

This particular day, as we watched the television, we didn't hear them come in.

"Well what do we have here?" Roger asked. I call him Roger, but I don't recall his actual name. He just seemed like a Roger.

"Jesus!" Mom yelped. "I told you two to stay in your room." She swayed and scratched at her arm.

"That true, kids?" Roger followed her lead. "You better listen to your mother, kids. Run along."

"Can we just finish this one, please?" Sam pleaded, though he knew the answer. I'm not even sure why he asked. He knew the answer, and he knew it might come with a belt.

"Are you talking back to me? Nobody talks back to Roger." Again, I don't remember if this was actually his name, but I do know he spoke in the third person the whole three months he stuck around. I guess I either hated him enough, or there were so many "hims" that I never cared to remember their names.

"No, I just..."

"Don't ever talk back to me!" Roger grabbed Sam by the arm and threw him a couple feet into the wall. He started kicking him and then unbuckled his belt, using it, buckle side at the end, as a whip. He hit Sam's arm a couple times, making him bleed.

I was crying hysterically, but I didn't dare say a word. I felt like a coward, but what could I do? Luckily, he left the beating at that. Some of them did far worse. Sam seemed like he was in pain, but he looked at me and gave me his best *I'm fine* face. We had facial cues for each other for when things like this would happen.

Roger grabbed Sam by his other arm, making him stand, and dragged him over to me, at which point, he grabbed my arm as well and started dragging us both up the stairs. We didn't fight him on this. We knew if we did, things would only get worse.

There was a linen closet in the upstairs hallway next to a dresser with a phone and a picture of our long passed grandmother on it. Mom kept the picture of Grandma on the table since she had given the table to her and my father as a wedding gift. If only Grandma knew how Mom would turn out, she may not have given her such nice things. Roger threw us into the tiny, crowded closet and shut the door.

Sam hugged me tight. He told me he was okay and then assured me we'd be alright.

"Shut up!" Roger yelled from the other side of the door. "I don't want to hear a word out of you. When you've learned your lesson, I'll let you out."

Just then, we heard a screeching across the floor. He had pushed the hall table in front of the door.

Panicked, Sam tried pushing against the door, but he couldn't get it to budge. Roger laughed proudly from the other side.

"You two be good now."

We heard his loud, clumsy steps down the stairs and then heard the muffled voices and giggling of him and my mother downstairs.

"Emily," Sam whispered, "don't cry; it will be okay." He held my hand. Thinking back on it, for nine years old, Sam was awfully grown up. I suppose he had to be.

A few hours had passed, and we had fallen asleep. It was dark inside the closet. The only light we could see was creeping in from beneath the door.

We were forced awake when we heard the front door slam shut. They were leaving. They were leaving and keeping us in this closet. When Mom went out, there was no telling sometimes when she'd be back. Panic began to set in again. Sam and I started screaming and pleading, and pushing and banging against the door. Our little bodies just couldn't make it move. The table was so heavy, made of cherry wood and marble, and it had a very heavy drawer full of crap Mom never threw away. We were trapped.

I whined to Sam how hungry and scared I was. He held my hand tight and kept telling me everything would be fine. To keep my mind off the fear, he told me a story of how one day he and I would have our own place far from Mom and her druggie boyfriends. He told me how happy we would be together, just me and him, and how no one would ever hurt us again, and he promised we would have a great big television set that we could watch cartoons on all day and all night. He said we could have a cat too. I loved cats, but my mother would never allow one in the house. Sam went on and on about how beautiful our life would be. This story would be told to me by Sam over and over for years to come, as this was not the only time we would be stuck in the dark closet together.

Just as he finished his story for the first time, he turned to stretch and hit his arm on one of the door hinges.

He yelled out in pain. I grabbed his arm and felt the warm liquid oozing from the wound Roger had made with his belt buckle.

"You have to lick it." I remember telling him.

"Gross," he said, "I don't want to lick it."

"You're supposed to. Cats do it. It helps." My eight year old brain remembered seeing it in a book once upon a time from one of the days I actually did go to school. "Here," I offered, "I'll do it."

Sam reluctantly gave over his arm.

So there, in the dark, tight space of the hallway closet, I licked my brother's wound. I had tasted blood before that day, but only my own. In the grand tradition of children wounding themselves on the playground, I had licked my knee after a spill once or twice. His blood was different, sweeter than my own. I liked it. It tasted like rust with sugar mixed in. It was somehow comforting, and it felt completely natural for me to be doing this for him. Cats do it after all; their saliva has an antiseptic. That's what I remembered reading, so I thought it would work the same for my brother. I know better now, but it doesn't take away from the memory of that experience.

Sam and I were in that closet for a day and a half. We had no food, no water, and nowhere to go to the bathroom. Of course, when they finally remembered we were in the closet, we got in trouble for messing ourselves, which resulted in a whole new set of consequences, but it didn't stop our mother and Roger and a plethora of other "men" from putting us back in there for hours, sometimes days, on end. On those days, Sam often went into that closet bleeding, as did I. Some of her boyfriends would leave me out of the beating part, but not many. We spent a lot of time in that closet. Each time, Sam and I would lick each other's wounds. It made us feel better; we felt closer and somehow safer. It was the only way we knew how to take care of each other in such a helpless situation. I'm not really sure when it happened, but at some point, we started craving that closeness, and we began sharing blood at times outside the darkness of that closet. It seemed innocent enough when we were children. I would scrape my knee, and he'd lick it for me, or he would cut his hand, and I would lick it for him. As teenagers it escalated. Both of us started cutting. Cutting ourselves gave us control over the pain, and we enjoyed it. No one else could decide what hurt us. We decided when and how, and we were always there to lap up each other's pain. Pain is different for everyone, but for us, it was a release, something we could manipulate and make our own; it was an invitation to feel something real for ourselves and for each other.

When Sam was eighteen, we decided to leave our mother. Sam had worked the three summers before his eighteenth birthday on a pig farm just outside the city. The farmer he worked for lived alone. His wife had passed several years before, and they never had children. Mr. Riley was the first genuinely nice man we'd ever known. He recognized Sam's timid behavior and the rotating bruises. He told Sam once that he had seen a belt or two in his day growing up, and he knew what it was like. He had a guest house on his farm and offered it to Sam in exchange for mucking, feeding, slaughtering and butchering, things Sam had grown quite skilled at. Mr. Riley also had an impressive corn field. While Sam could stay in that house in exchange for caring for the pigs and seeing to their timely butchering, he would still be paid a regular wage for minding the crop. Sam explained to Mr. Riley that he couldn't leave me behind, and being the kind man he was, he let Sam bring me with him.

We were overjoyed to leave our mother in her drunken stupor. One night, while she was out with Roger number forty-six, we packed up all that we could fit into Sam's bomber car, started it up, and never looked back. We had never been happier. We finally had that house we'd always dreamed about, just me and him. There was a cat too, several cats actually. Mr. Riley had a large group of barn cats. They weren't too friendly, but of course, in order to make our dream complete, I began trying to tame one immediately. One cat in particular took to me fairly quickly. After a few weeks, I finally convinced her to come in the house. Little by little, she warmed to the idea of being inside and letting me pet her. By the second month, her and I were great friends.

Life on the farm was wonderful. I helped Sam with some of his chores, and Mr. Riley was always so kind and appreciative.

Though we were feeling true happiness and peace for the first time in our lives, Sam and I still had the strong desire to share blood, and so we did. If Mr. Riley knew we did this, he never let on that he knew. He and Sam worked a lot together during the day, but only during daylight was he really around. He was always back in his house for dinner, and he enjoyed his solitude, keeping to himself at night.

A year had passed since we'd moved onto the farm. It was the end of July, and the heat was almost unbearable. Mr. Riley had entrusted Sam with the care of his farm while he went to visit family for a couple months. It was a huge responsibility, but he had faith in my brother.

Not long before Mr. Riley left, Sam had started dating. I had mixed feelings about him seeing women. I wanted him to be happy, but I couldn't stand the idea of him loving someone else. I didn't want him to leave me. He knew I was hurt, and so he suggested that I try it as well. Though I was extremely apprehensive and didn't feel good about the idea, I decided I should give it a try for Sam's sake. Only problem was, I didn't know anyone. No one had ever asked me out, and I didn't know where to begin trying to meet people. Sam was more social than I was. He was always going into the city and going to bars. I was scared to leave home. Besides, what was really out there for me? A Roger?

Knowing it was next to impossible for me to approach anyone in person, I thought I would try a dating site. We didn't have internet on the farm, so I went into the city and set up a profile for myself on a dating website at the city library. The whole idea was terrifying. I'd never been on a date before. I didn't think anyone would even want to go out with me. I lied up and down in my profile to make myself seem more interesting and put together than I was. I didn't even use my real name. Emily seemed so boring at the time, so I went with Vivian. For some reason that sounded like a worldly name, an experienced name. Twenty minutes after I'd completed my fantasy profile, I received my first message. His name was Teddy. He was in his junior year at the university and, according to his profile, looking for someone he could really fall in love with. I was sure that someone wouldn't be me, but it was the only message I'd received thus far. It read: *Nice to meet you, Vivian. I am new to this internet dating thing, but it's so hard to meet nice, normal people these days. I would love to get together for a drink if you are free. Let me know what's good for you. -Teddy.*

Normal people? That could be me. A drink? I could do that. I was only eighteen then, but most of the bars in town didn't card. At least that's what my brother had told me. I chewed on my thumb nail a good five minutes before responding.

Sure. I wrote. *Sounds great. Tonight works for me. I'll meet you at Lane's Bar and Grill at 8?* Looking back, replying right away and meeting with him the very same day does seem a little desperate, but again, I had never done this.

He replied promptly with an *ok.* I was so excited and completely scared out of my mind. I showed up an hour early and sat nervously at the bar. I had attempted to put on makeup, something I hadn't had much experience with, which probably showed with my very bold choice of colors, over use of blush, and lack of technique with lipstick application. Nevertheless, I was doing this. I chewed anxiously on my swizzle straw. I had ordered a long island, which I'd promptly sucked down. The bar tender didn't card me, either because he felt sorry for me looking like a mismatched nervous clown, or because my brother was right, they really don't care as long as you're paying.

"Vivian?" a confused voice asked from behind me.

I swiveled around on the stool to greet him.

"Teddy? Hi!" I stuck out my clammy right hand. I was pretty sure that's the appropriate way to greet a blind date.

"Hi," he said as he smiled sweetly. "May I sit?" He moved toward the stool next to me. He seemed nervous too. He motioned for the bartender. "Two more of whatever she's having."

"Oh," I said, smiling and giggling, "thank you."

"Sure."

We sat in silence for only a moment, but it seemed like an eternity. I would look at him and then quickly look away and giggle. I felt completely out of my element.

A few drinks more, and everything had changed. We were having a real conversation and seemed to be getting along really well. He kept ordering me drink after drink while he carefully sipped away at his one glass. He was so nice and really good looking. What was I so nervous about before? This was wonderful. He told me all about school and where he saw himself in five years, settled down in a great big house with a wife and kids, and I told him, sparing the bloodletting details, about my living on the farm with my brother and how beautiful it was. I let it slip that my brother was also in the city that night and that the farmer was out of town.

Being the prince that he was, Teddy offered to drive me home. I didn't have my own car, so I normally would take the bus to the last stop on the edge of town and then walk the mile back to the farm, but he said it was too dangerous for a pretty girl like me to be walking home in the dark like that. He called me pretty. I'd never heard anyone say that before. My brother had told me I was beautiful, but he was my blood, and I always thought he was obligated to say nice things. Coming from a stranger, it sounded so amazing. I could almost believe it. Having him pay me such undivided attention, I felt pretty.

By the time we left, I had downed five long islands. He let me lean on him as he directed me toward the car. He'd only had one drink, so he was more than capable of getting me home.

I told him how to get to the farm. He pulled his car up to the guest house and cut the engine.

"So," he said sweetly, "there's no one home right now? Why don't we go inside?"

"We better call it a night. I have to get up early." I was too embarrassed to tell him that I was feeling sick from all the alcohol. "Thank you for driving me home."

"Sure, no problem. How about a good night kiss then?"

"Uh…" I hesitated. I hadn't ever kissed anyone before, and I didn't want my first kiss to happen while my head was swirling.

"Come on," he insisted, reaching over. "It's a million degrees out. Why don't you take off this jacket?" he questioned as he pawed at me.

"No, wait." I really wanted out of the car. I tugged at my seatbelt and finally got it loose. My hand then began desperately searching for the door handle, but I couldn't quite find it.

He hadn't given up, and pretty soon, he was all over me. I was trying to push him away with one hand and keep searching for my way out with the other.

"Come on, Vivian. Just give me a try. I've been so nice to you. Can't you be nice to me?" Hearing him say that name aloud instantly made me regret my decision to use it. He laughed as he ripped at my tights. I had worn black stalkings and the jacket to cover up the scarring on my legs and arms. He tore a hole in the stalking over my right thigh and gasped as he saw the damaged flesh he had just exposed. "Oh," he exclaimed, "you're a freak."

I was horrified, but for some reason, this revelation made him smile.

"You never said you were a freak." He laughed. "Now come on over here." He kept pulling at me. I tried my best to fend him off, but it seemed like I was failing. My stomach was turning at a new speed, and my head was pounding. Tears were beginning to stream down my painted face. I'm sure I was screaming, but he didn't seem to mind.

Just as he started working at my jacket, the driver's side door swung open. All I could see were two large hands grabbing at Teddy. One hand choked him by his shirt collar, and the other was wrapped up in his hair. Teddy was pulled swiftly from the car.

I felt this giant relief sweep over me. I could breathe again. The lights from the porch cast a slight glow over the car. As my hero turned toward the glow, I recognized him as my brother. He must have gotten home before us. I loved him even more in this moment.

I heard Teddy gasping and pleading on the grass next to the car. I climbed out the open door and stood behind Sam. He was pulling his blade from his pocket. Teddy saw this and scrambled to get up. My brother knocked him back to the ground and kicked him in the stomach, taking his breath away from him and silencing his screams.

Behind us, I could hear the screams of the pigs from the barn. They sounded so much like humans sometimes. I often found solace in their cries. There was something so soothing about the way they let out their energy that way. It wasn't a cry of fear or frustration; it seemed like such a positive and happy release. Us humans usually scream out of anger or terror. I envied those pigs. They never knew what real fear was. Even their slaughters, quick as they were, seemed so peaceful. They never knew it was coming. Sam and I never had that luxury.

Teddy lay on the grass, fear in his eyes, a fear I had seen many times before, a fear I had no doubt just displayed myself in his car when he attacked me. I was happy to see him like this. He deserved it. All men like him deserved it. If only all the Rogers of the world could experience this moment with him. As the blade glistened in the faint light, the moment felt more and more perfect.

"Do it, Sam," I encouraged my brother.

Sam took a small angry breath and lunged toward Teddy, jabbing his blade into Teddy's throat. Sam pulled the knife out of him. Teddy put his hands to his throat and tried desperately to stop the bleeding. I smiled as the life began to fade from his face. His hands fell limply below his wound. There was a slight gurgling sound as the last of the air escaped from the hole Sam had made. Teddy was gone.

My brother turned to me and hugged me tightly.

"God, Em, are you okay?"

"I will be. Thank you." I didn't want to let him go.

"Shit!" He yelled, his voice filled with concern. "What if someone comes looking for this guy? What if they find us?"

"They won't. I... uh..." I was so wrapped up in what had just happened, I had almost forgotten how we'd gotten there in the first place. "I used a fake name, and the website, on the website, there was no picture. I set up an email account, but it was just for the site, and I didn't use my name. No one will know it was me. I'll go to the library tomorrow and take it all down. How would they know?" Adrenaline circulated through my body. I felt so alive, so invincible.

"Okay, good." Sam seemed to be on the same page. He didn't seem upset or shaken by what he'd done. He seemed completely rational. He wanted to make sure we were in the clear. "His car... what about his car?"

"The pond!" I looked toward the pond. It had to be deep enough. It was definitely large enough. I knew no one would ever find it there. Mr. Riley fished in it every now and then during the summer, but he never fished the north side of it. It was perfect.

"Yeah. That could work. Okay."

We both stared down at the body. His shirt was soaked in blood. As I gazed down, I found myself lusting after his warm blood. I wanted it. I needed it. I glanced at my brother, and he seemed to be thinking the same thing. It was strange. We'd never thought of taking in someone else's blood before, but somehow it seemed so right. He was there now for our disposal.

Sam turned to me with a longing in his eye. Our desires met in silence. Neither of us said a word as he bent down to pick up Teddy. He threw him over his shoulder and started off toward the slaughterhouse. I followed just behind with boiling anticipation.

I watched gleefully as Sam skillfully disrobed and prepped my assailant for butcher. It was all so exciting. Teddy's skin was placed in a bucket to the side and would later be given to the pigs. That might seem odd, but pigs are omnivores and will literally eat anything. Teddy was cut into perfect pieces. He was so beautiful and tender.

Once Sam had cut him up satisfactorily, we retreated to the guest house and pan fried part of our kill. Sitting down to the table, we were both nervous but equally excited. We cut and took our first bites at the same time. It was amazing. We'd never had anything like it. It tasted like vengeance, and vengeance was sweet. With every bite, we were satisfying a deep and long ignored hunger. Every morsel filled a hole that our mother and every Roger had ever made within our souls. It was exquisite; The most perfect meal we'd ever had. After dinner, Sam and I went back to the slaughterhouse to distribute the rest of the body to the pigs. The poor creatures squealed in delight. They seemed to enjoy it as much as we did. There was such poetry in the air. Sam and I worked together in silence. We'd catch each other's glance every now and then and just smile. So simple. So perfect.

That night, we showered together. It wasn't sexual; it was pure comfort. We held each other as the hot water ran over our bodies. I could feel his heart beating through his skin, and he could feel mine. They were in synch. The rhythm was intoxicating. We just stood, together, as one being.

Once clean, we went back to the car and drove it to the edge of the pond. We put it in neutral and pushed it in. As the car sank into the dark water, my brother held my hand. We burned Teddy's clothes, keeping his phone out, and then went to bed and slept a full night's sound sleep.

The next day, Sam drove me into town so I could destroy my dating profile. I put Teddy's phone in a trash can by the coffee shop. I didn't have my own cell phone, but I knew enough about them to know some of them have GPS devices. That was that. There was no evidence I had ever been with Teddy. Sure, the bartender saw us together, but I wasn't exactly memorable, and he'd never seen me before, and if he did remember anything, it would have been Teddy with a drunk innocent girl named Vivian. No one knew Emily.

A couple weeks passed, and Sam and I started to feel the hunger again. We discussed it, and I decided to go back to the library and set up a new profile. We set rules for the dates. We only wanted to target the men that would turn out to be a Roger or a Teddy. The interesting thing was, all the men I met on the websites were Rogers or Teddys. I always posted under a fake name, using a different name every time, and I always used a different computer to make sure no one could pin point the IP address. I may not have graduated high school, but since moving to the farm, I had watched quite a few criminal investigation shows. I would rotate on the computers at the library and the internet café. I only dated every few weeks, and once I was sure that my date was a slime ball looking for a one night stand, I would get him out to the farm where Sam could take over. By my third date, Mr. Riley was back home, so I had to be more careful about bringing the men back. I had them come around the corn field to the back side of the guest house. That way, Mr. Riley wouldn't be able to see the headlights. Sam would get the pigs riled up before he'd approach the car, and that way Mr. Riley wouldn't hear the men scream, and since the slaughterhouse was out of sight of Mr. Riley's bedroom and living room windows, he never saw the lights on.

And so was born our routine. I would meet the guys for drinks, always at a different place, or on different nights when they had different staff. Without fail, the Roger would offer me a ride, and so long as his car was a late model and/or didn't have a GPS or low jack system, I would get in. I would get him to the farm, we'd wait for the guy to get a little pushy, which, unfortunately for them, they always did, and then Sam would come to my rescue. We'd then take him to the slaughterhouse, cut him up, put our meat aside and then feed the rest to our friends in the barn. We'd put the car in neutral and send it into the pond, and Sam would dispose of the guy's clothes and personal belongings. The cell phones were always taken back into town later on and put in various places. It was absolute perfection, that is until we ran out of space on the north side of the pond. We had twelve sunken cars on that side, and were running dangerously close to exposing ourselves to the kind farmer, but we couldn't stop.

So here we are today. The last two cars, we've swept clean and left burned out in remote places, making it look like theft. So far, out of our fourteen Rogers, only three of them have made the paper as missing persons. I suppose everyone shared the same warm and fuzzy feelings we had for the others. No one has missed them so far. We had always thought society would be much better off without all the Rogers and the Teddys, and it seems the world agrees with us.

As for Sam and I, all we can do is the best we can for each other. We have never been happier, and our love is unbreakable. We've made a pact that if anyone tries to break us up, we just simply won't go on as individuals. Death doesn't frighten Sam and me. In fact, we embrace death. When she comes for us, we will be ready. For now, we are exploring the joys in life and nature. Sam is keeping himself busy with the crop and learning more tools of the trade; and me, well, I have a date tonight.

THE JOYS OF MOTHERHOOD

I held my husband's hand tightly as we waited in Dr. Stanley's office. I tried to keep myself distracted, so I didn't have to think of the possibilities. What if the in vitro hadn't worked? What would we do? We had spoken about adoption, but we really wanted to try on our own. My eyes darted around the room as they had done on so many visits before. I glanced once more at the framed diplomas and the family photos, hung proudly on the walls. This whole process hadn't been so bad. At least trying gave us hope, but we were running out of options. It was all the waiting that seemed most difficult. Sitting in that chair, waiting for lab result after lab result was terrifying and exhausting to say the least.

I heard the door knob turning, and I gripped Daniel's hand even harder. I'm sure I was hurting him, but knowing my fear, he let me wrench his hand without flinching.

Dr. Stanley rounded the desk and took his seat across from us. He was holding a manila colored folder in his left hand. He carefully placed it on the desk. Normally by this point, he was already opening the chart to re-examine the pages inside and review the bad news.

He put his hands together and calmly put them on the cherry wood desk top. A smile began to spread across his aged face.

"Well, Corporal Lundy, Mrs. Lundy," he addressed my husband and me, "I am very pleased to say that the procedure has indeed worked. All of your efforts and patience have paid off. Congratulations, Rachel. You are pregnant."

I let out a squeal, that I'm sure could be heard throughout the entire building and probably across the entire base.

"Oh my god, Daniel! This is amazing!" I jumped up as he did, and we held each other tightly. Tears began streaming down my face. Daniel pulled away, and I could see his eyes were welling up also.

"Wow, thank you, Dr. Stanley," Daniel said, reaching for the doctor's hand.

"Yes, I'm glad we could help make your family more complete. With that said, there are a few things we need to discuss. Please," he said as he motioned for us to sit back in our chairs. "Now, Rachel, I know you are excited, but this is a very delicate time. Sometimes within the first trimester, after a successful in vitro procedure, there can be complications. I don't want either of you to worry. We will be keeping a very close eye on you as time goes on, but I would like to take extra special measures to ensure everything goes well. I would like to schedule weekly visits just so I can make sure you and the baby continue in proper health."

"Weekly?" I questioned. "That seems excessive. None of the books or publications I read said anything about weekly checkups. Is there something wrong or any reason I should worry?"

"No, no, of course not," the doctor reassured. "It's just that we want to take the best care we can of our soldiers and their families. I know how long you have waited for this baby, and I want to handle this pregnancy with the utmost care. So, please, let's see Denise on the way out, and we'll work out a schedule for your checkups."

"Alright," I agreed, "you know best. Thank you."

"I know we've been over everything several times in the last few months, but do either of you have any more questions before you go?" the doctor asked kindly.

"No," Daniel answered. He looked to me to be sure I didn't either. I shook my head no and smiled and he continued, "I think that's it Doc. Thank you so much. You have no idea how happy we are."

"Well I'm happy that I am able to be a part of this great moment." Dr. Stanley stood to escort us toward the front.

I wiped my joyous tears from my face, grabbed my bag and Daniel's hand, and we walked in a happy daze toward the front of Dr. Stanley's office.

"Denise," Dr. Stanley whispered, so as not to disturb the calm in the waiting room, "please assist Mrs. Lundy with her appointment schedule. I want to do weeklies with her. Thank you. Alright," Dr. Stanley said, turning back to us, "if you have any questions, please feel free to call the office; otherwise, I will see you next week for your first checkup." He smiled, grabbed a pile of charts from the bin on Denise's desk, and turned to go back toward his office.

Daniel and I didn't talk the entire ride home. We were both completely consumed with thought. Daniel drove the car up into the driveway, put it in park, turned off the ignition, and stared blankly at the garage door in front of us. Then at the same time, we turned to each other and began cheering and laughing with excitement. He jumped out of the driver's seat and ran around to my side, throwing open the passenger door. He unbuckled my seatbelt and grabbed me up from my seat.

"What are you doing?" I said, laughing as he shut the car door with his foot and toted me toward the front door.

"I am carrying my wife and my baby into the house. You, love, are a princess, and today, I do whatever you ask." He kissed my forehead and fumbled with the lock for a moment.

"Whatever I ask? Well that sounds like a pretty sweet deal." I continued giggling as we went inside.

That night he made me dinner, and we discussed how and when to tell everyone our incredible news. We both thought the most logical thing, of course, would be to wait a while longer before making the announcement, just in case something went wrong, but we decided to lean toward optimism and let our excitement out of the bag and call everyone we knew.

My mother would be the first to know. I couldn't wait to share the news. I had always dreamed of the day Daniel and I would be expecting, and my mother would help me make all the plans, and decorate the nursery, and help me pick out baby clothes, and let me in on all the secrets to great motherhood over lunches. Unfortunately, being a military wife usually means that your family isn't all that close by, and in this case, my family was two thousand miles away. Daniel's family wasn't quite as far, but far enough. His mother passed away when he was twelve, and his father and step-mother lived about eight hours from the base. I had a little sister, who being sixteen, still lived at home with my mother, and Daniel had two brothers, one younger, also still at home with his family, and one older, who also happened to be in the military and at the time stationed in Germany.

Though we were bursting at the seams to let everyone in on our joy, we decided it could at least wait until morning. Daniel carried me up the stairs to our bedroom, passing the room where our son or daughter would soon be sleeping, and we got ready for bed. That night, I slept so soundly. I hadn't slept that well in months, but knowing that we were finally getting the family we'd always wanted put me at such ease.

A week had already passed. A week full of giddy nursery planning and baby name tossing went by in a flash. It was already time for my first prenatal checkup with Dr. Stanley.

I sat on the examining table in my oh so uncomfortable gown, waiting for Dr. Stanley to reappear. He'd already checked my vitals and insisted on drawing blood for some sort of work up. He mentioned something about my results from my previous visit showing signs of a potassium deficiency and possible anemia, and he needed to do more labs to be sure. I sat on the table shifting from one side to the other nervously. The paper crackled beneath me every time I moved. My ankles were linked together as were my nervous hands. I wished Daniel could have been there with me, but he had to work that day.

There was a slight knock at the door, and then Dr. Stanley appeared back in the room. He was holding what seemed to be a cartoonishly large syringe. It was filled with a bluish liquid. I hated needles. Having my blood drawn and being injected with hormones all these months was bad enough, but something about this syringe made me very uneasy.

Dr. Stanley, noticing my anxiety, began explaining the needle's purpose. "Okay, Rachel. We will have to wait a few days for these new labs to come back before we know for sure how low the levels of potassium are in your body, but we have been able to determine with a drop test that you are most definitely anemic, and to a fairly serious degree. You may have noticed yourself feeling more fatigued than usual."

"Sure," I offered, "but I had just assumed it was all the stress and excitement."

"Well, unfortunately, it likely has more to do with this iron deficiency, so, I am going to start you on some iron tablets and this here injection will just ensure that your body absorbs and stores the iron properly."

"Uh..." This made me extremely uncomfortable. I had never heard of such a thing, but then again, I wasn't the doctor in the room.

"I completely understand your hesitation, Rachel. It's perfectly natural to feel uneasy about all this. It can be scary, especially since this is your first pregnancy, but trust me. This will have you feeling better in no time, and the baby really does need proper nutrients to stay healthy."

"I'm sorry, Dr. Stanley. I guess you're right. I just really hate needles." I laughed nervously and smiled at my trusted doctor.

"I know you do. Don't worry, this will be quick and painless." He took the needle from the tray and removed the cap. I turned my head to the right and closed my eyes as he raised the sleeve of my gown and pushed the needle through the skin on my left shoulder. I bit my lip as I felt the liquid enter my muscle. He withdrew the needle.

"Wow," I said, "that really burns. Is that normal?"

"Yes, sorry. I guess it wasn't completely painless," he attempted to joke and smiled charmingly. "It may sting for a little while, but like I said, you'll feel better in no time."

"Alrighty." I chuckled after him and rubbed my shoulder.

He turned and put the syringe in the hazardous waste bin and peeled off and threw his gloves in after it.

"Oh," I said, remembering the iron supplements, "the iron tablets, I can get those in the vitamin aisle, right?"

"No need, Rachel." The doctor reached into his white coat pocket and pulled out an orange prescription bottle. "Here you go. Just take one a day, preferably at the same time each day. Now, I should have your labs back in the next few days. At your next appointment we will check your iron again and discuss the results of your potassium test. You may need to have that shot I just gave you again."

"It's not something that could harm the baby is it?" I asked. "I really don't mean to be so on edge, but I really don't want to put any unnecessary chemicals in my body if it could potentially harm him or her." I grabbed my abdomen.

Dr. Stanley first looked annoyed by my question but then quickly turned his expression to a concerned smile.

"No, dear," he said sweetly, "this is for both your benefit. The injection is simply an additive designed to make sure your body properly stores and distributes important vitamins to yourself and your baby. It doesn't have any harmful side effects. Guaranteed." He smiled again and gently put his hand on my sore shoulder. This was reassuring. Why was I questioning this man anyway? He was after all the miracle worker that gave me and my husband a chance at parenthood. Without him, I wouldn't have been pregnant.

"Of course." I smiled back. "I will do whatever you think is best. Thank you."

"Okay then, Rachel. Go ahead and get dressed and confirm your appointment for next week with Denise. I'll see you next week." He opened the door to exit but then turned with a final thought, "and don't forget, if you need anything or have any questions, please, don't hesitate."

"Thank you, doctor." I exchanged a smile, and as the door shut, I peeled myself off the paper and quickly dressed. My arm was already feeling better.

I arrived home that afternoon to find Daniel waiting for me. He normally didn't come home until after six or seven.

"Hey, honey! What are you doing home?" I walked toward him, arms open for a hug.

He reached his arms out, and we met in the hallway.

"Well," he began, "we had sort of a situation today, and the Staff Sergeant sent my team home."

"Oh my god. Is it serious?" I was ready to grab my emergency duffle bag from the coat closet.

"No, nothing to worry about. They're starting a new *project*." The way he said it, I knew it was need to know only, which meant he wasn't privy to the concept yet. "And since it's in the beginning stages, they only required one team of engineers and a couple extra hands. All it really means is I have the rest of the day off to spend with you."

"Well, I am glad you're here, but when my husband, the nuclear weapons specialist, comes home in the middle of the day because of a *situation* I get a little nervous, so next time you might want to lead with the everything's okay part." I smiled and kissed him.

"Ah, yes, sorry." He chuckled and hugged me tight, pressing against my arm which I now noticed was still a little tender.

"Ouch!" I pulled back from his embrace.

"Sorry, you okay? Did I hurt you?"

"No, I got a shot with a giant horse needle today." I rubbed my arm in remembrance.

"Why? Is everything okay? What did the doctor say?"

"Yeah, I'm fine; the baby's fine. I just need to take some iron supplements and probably eat more bananas. My potassium might be a little low, but Dr. Stanley says it's nothing to be too concerned about, and this shot is supposed to help my body hang on to the nutrients or something, so all should be well."

"That's great, babe. I'm really glad to hear that everything is okay with little Tucker in there." He rubbed my belly jovially.

"Yeah, about that, I'm not too stoked on that name, but we'll work on it. I mean, what if it's a girl?"

"We're still naming her Tucker." He smiled and kissed my forehead. "Come on. I'll take you to dinner."

The next few weeks were a little stressful. Daniel was becoming frustrated with his work. His unit had been moved to another building. The new project he had announced weeks before had apparently required the larger work space, and they decided to move that project to Daniel's building, so his team had to move a couple structures over. His access to that building was revoked, and he was never clued in to what sort of weapon they were working on. He was used to being in the loop, but he kept to his own project and focused on the work of his own unit.

I kept my weekly appointments with Dr. Stanley. In addition to the iron supplements he had given me, I was taking pills to increase my potassium. Dr. Stanley was very accommodating. He never wrote a prescription, but would rather fill and give me the supplements himself. He was still concerned about my mineral absorption, so he insisted on weekly injections. I was getting used to the giant needle by now, but it made me a little uneasy that I had to continue with the shots. I couldn't find anything in any of my books or on the internet about this sort of thing, but I was feeling great, and Dr. Stanley was very convincing.

One night, at six weeks into my pregnancy, I woke to an excruciating pain in my lower abdomen. I could barely breathe, it was so strong. I woke Daniel and asked him to call Dr. Stanley, who was glad to answer the call. He advised not to go to the hospital and that he would be right over.

Once the doctor arrived, the pain had already lessened considerably. Daniel waited eagerly on the opposite side of the room as the doctor came to my side of the bed to examine me and ask about my pain. After I explained what had happened, he checked my vitals and felt around my abdomen.

"Well, Rachel," Dr. Stanley said, exhaling as he let my shirt back down over my stomach, "it looks to me like everything is perfectly normal. I know that was scary, but I'm positive it all comes back to the potassium deficiency we've been dealing with. It was just a cramp. Although no doubt extremely painful, it's nothing to worry about, and the baby should be fine."

"But," I said, confused, "I've been taking the supplements, and I've had all those shots..."

"Yes, but perhaps we should up your dosage on your next visit. It's really not uncommon for this sort of thing to happen. When is your next appointment?"

"Wednesday at ten," I replied, rubbing the area he had just examined.

"Well, that's only a few days from now. If you're more comfortable, we can move up your appointment, but I'm confident that everything is fine."

"No, that's alright, if you're sure." I was worried, no matter what he said. It didn't feel like a simple charley horse to me, but then again, what did I know about medicine?

"Okay then, we'll keep your appointment, and I will do an ultrasound to make sure the baby's development is on track, and you'll see everything is just fine. In the meantime, let's do something more for your potassium."

"Well," I offered, "after our last appointment, I had read a little about this on the internet, and I found that too much potassium can be dangerous. I also got a list of foods that can help bring up potassium and iron levels naturally." I was proud of my self-education.

"Well, in all honesty, the supplement you're on right now is a very low dose, so I would like to have you start taking two of those pills per day. It's not dangerous at all so long as you take it properly. I happen to have some extra with me now. In addition to your iron supplements, take two of these per day, and hopefully, the cramping will get better." He reached into his bag and pulled out another orange bottle for me. "Now, to be perfectly frank with you, Rachel, you will still experience pains like these from time to time, it's normal, but this really should help."

I looked to Daniel with concern. He moved around to the other side of the bed to take the bottle from the doctor.

"Thank you Dr. Stanley, and thank you so much for coming out here in the middle of the night. We appreciate it." Daniel shook the doctor's hand, and the two of them began to walk toward the bedroom door.

"Alright, Rachel, you get some rest, and I will see you on Wednesday," Dr. Stanley noted as he continued out behind Daniel.

I just lay there, trying to absorb the information, trying to be okay with the idea that this kind of pain was normal. I had read about women experiencing muscle cramps during pregnancy, but this pain was so intense. It felt like I was being stabbed in the stomach. Though I explained it this way to Dr. Stanley, he insisted it was cramping.

I started taking the pills Dr. Stanley gave me, and the pain didn't come back that week, so I thought everything was okay. I went ahead with my Wednesday appointment. Being at six weeks, this was our first ultra sound, so Daniel came with me. Dr. Stanley showed us our baby, and we squealed in excitement. The fetus was so small, we really didn't know what we were looking at, but we were excited all the same. The doctor assured me everything looked as it should and that the baby was developing normally. He gave me my weekly injection, and Daniel and I went on with our day, both content that everything was fine.

The next couple months were up and down. Daniel had adjusted to the transition at work and was back on track with his team. I, however, was experiencing pain fairly frequently and having a difficult time sleeping. It only happened at night when I was most relaxed, something the doctor advised was especially normal of severe muscle spasm. I still wasn't satisfied with the charley horse theory. To me, it felt like someone was carving my insides. It would happen in various places in my abdomen, and afterward, it seemed to cause a lot of daily discomfort. The daytime pains the doctor explained as gas. He said it was very common to experience gastritis during pregnancy and gave me a list of foods to avoid and a new pill to alleviate some of the discomfort. I had also been experiencing the weirdest craving for rare burgers and raw fish. Dr. Stanley suggested that red meat is a very ordinary craving for pregnant women, especially those in need of more iron, but he of course advised to stay away from sushi because of the risks involved with mercury and the various bacteria in raw fish. I entertained the thought of raw meat often, but I hadn't yet given in to it. The idea was something that would have repulsed me before I was pregnant, and I tried to keep that in mind every time I thought of biting into an uncooked steak. At that time, I stuck to cooked foods.

Another two months had passed, and my mother came for a visit. At nearly five months pregnant, I was showing and couldn't wait for her to see my belly. I was also ecstatic to have her around to help. The nursery had a long way to go, and I wanted to pick her brain about so many things, and the phone conversations just weren't cutting it. She left my little sister, Amber, home with my dad for the week. I had really wanted to see Amber and my dad, but my sister couldn't miss school, and my father hated to fly.

As soon as my mother got there, the energy in the house sped up. She had idea after idea about the baby's room, and, of course, I begged her to try and talk Daniel out of the whole "Tucker" thing. Poor Daniel. Once you get a mother and daughter going, it's every man for themselves, especially when it came to me and my mom. We were best friends and both full of opinions.

The first day we just caught up. I told her what little I knew about Daniel's work; he wasn't at liberty to share much, even with me, something I was well aware of and made peace with before we got married; and I divulged all the current happenings in my own day to day. I also told her about the intense pains I was having, but how the doctor had explained them as normal cramping, and she seemed to agree with that explanation. She told me that a lot of pregnant women experience cramping, which I already knew, but hearing her say it after I told her how bad it was, put my mind at ease a little. She caught me up on how Amber was doing and told me all about my father's decision to go into birdhouse construction. He was recently retired and bored out of his mind, so he found solace in his birdhouses. He had even sold a few of them.

The second day, Mom and I went on an adventure off base and into town to do a little paint and wallpaper shopping.

Staring at all the different patterns made this all seem so amazing, so real. I was having a baby, and I was finally getting to choose décor for that child's room.

"So," my mother said as she held up paint samples, "are we going to find out the sex this week? Or are we just going to paint the room pink and hope that if it's a boy he can handle the ridicule?"

"Part of me really wants to wait, you know? The element of surprise... the other part of me knows I did always hate surprises, so I'm a little torn." I smiled and picked up a sage green sample.

"Okay, okay, I'm not going to pressure you, but, it would be a lot easier for me to spoil my first grandchild pre-birth if I knew if I should be buying dresses or overalls. If it were me, I would have wanted to know already."

"No. I'm going to wait. I am. I am going to wait," I said, sounding completely unsure. I laughed at my own indecisiveness. I really wanted to know, but Daniel and I had agreed to wait. "Yep, that's all there is to it. I'm going to wait."

"Well then, what are we going to do about the room?" She was still holding pink swatches. I would have never considered painting the room pink anyway, even I was having ten girls.

"I am thinking something simple and suitable for either. I really like this green. It's kind of soothing, and I'm thinking I like that jungle theme for trim." I pointed to a wallpaper border with monkeys and elephants.

"You know, I absolutely hate doing wallpaper, but I think you're right. This is pretty perfect." My mother smiled and grabbed my swatch as she trotted off to find someone to help us get our supplies.

After we gathered our painting materials, we headed to this little baby boutique I'd been dying to go to and picked out a crib and a rocking chair. My mom was such a big help. Daniel had been so busy on base, he hadn't had the time to help with much of the preparation, and I really didn't want to do it alone.

A few cans of paint and a couple home furnishings richer, and about four hundred dollars poorer, we decided to call it a day and went home to prepare dinner. Mom offered to make her famous lasagna for Daniel and me. He came home to our chatter and the smell of good food. He was delighted to see me so happy. Sweet man that my husband was, he even offered to clean up the kitchen after dinner so my mom and I could continue to visit.

The next day, I took my mom to my doctor's appointment. I really wanted her to meet Dr. Stanley, and I had hoped to get a new sonogram picture for her to take home with her. I had already set up the sonogram with Dr. Stanley, and I was sure he wouldn't mind my mother coming along.

I sat on the exam table paper once again and let it crinkle beneath me. This time, I was far more comfortable as my mom was there with me. After a slight knock at the door and hearing me say I was ready, Dr. Stanley appeared in the room.

"Oh, hello!" He looked surprised and a little disappointed as he addressed my mother. He turned his concerned gaze to me. "Rachel, I didn't know you were bringing a guest."

"Yes, Dr. Stanley, this is my mother, Deirdre," I said with a smile, hoping that it was alright she was there. I hadn't thought it would be a problem.

"Pleased to meet you, Deirdre." He forced a smile and a polite tone and extended his hand in welcome.

"And you." My mother shook his hand as she examined his face. She seemed displeased with his odd reaction to her being there.

Dr. Stanley soon regained his usual demeanor and began with the checkup. After the normal weekly routine and series of questions, he asked me to lie back for the ultrasound. He squirted the cold lubricant on my belly and began to move the transducer around. He pointed to the image on the screen.

"You can come around here, Deirdre, to have a look at your grandchild," Dr. Stanley advised as he motioned for my mom to come around the other side of me.

"Wow," my mom said. She started welling up. "Look at that."

"Rachel, you're sure you don't want to know the sex?" he asked. He'd asked the previous week when I set up the ultrasound appointment, but I had told him we were waiting.

"No, I promised Daniel we'd wait." I let out a sigh. The anticipation was driving me crazy, but we had an agreement that we'd be surprised.

"Okay then." Dr. Stanley moved the instrument around to get the best image and then optioned to print from the keyboard. "There you go. Your first picture of your grandchild," Dr. Stanley said as he handed the print out to my mother.

"Thank you." She wiped a single tear from her cheek and gave me a hug. "My first grandbaby!"

"Alright, well, everything looks great, Rachel. I'm just going to go grab your shot, and we'll be set."

The doctor left the room and shut the door behind him.

"So, what do you think?" I turned to my mom.

"What do I think? I think I'm going have a heart attack. I'm so excited!" She couldn't stop smiling.

"No, Ma, what do you think about Dr. Stanley?"

"Oh, well, I'm not sure he was too happy to see me for whatever reason. That's a little strange, but he is the man that made this miracle possible, so I guess I have to like him, right?" She shrugged and laughed.

I laughed too and then sat up in anticipation of the horse needle.

My mom looked away when Dr. Stanley stuck the needle in my arm. It seemed to bother her almost as much as it bothered me.

"Now what is this shot for again?" she quizzed.

"Well, Rachel has had a difficult time sustaining the proper level of nutrients she needs to maintain the health of herself and the baby, so this injection essentially works as a sort of mineral sponge once inside her blood stream. It holds onto and helps properly distribute the vitamins and minerals she is getting from her supplements. It ensures she gets the most from her pills." Dr. Stanley turned after his mini tutorial and deposited the syringe in the hazardous waste container as he always did.

"Huh," my mother replied, "I've never heard of such a thing."

"Rest assured, it's a very common practice," Dr. Stanley affirmed.

"Well," my mother said, seemingly unconvinced, "you're the doctor."

Dr. Stanley forced another smile in her direction and then turned to me once more to remind me to confirm my day and time for the next week with Denise at the front desk, something I had done seventeen times before. I told him I certainly would. We said our goodbyes and exchanged our pleasantries, and he disappeared back through the door.

On the way home, I could tell that my mother was holding something back.

"What's wrong?" I asked, trying to keep my focus on the road ahead.

"I don't want to upset you, but something just doesn't seem right with Dr. Stanley." She was pursing her lips like she always did when she was upset.

"What do you mean?"

"Well, these injections you're getting make me nervous. And all the supplements. It just seems like a lot. I mean, your poor body. And he wasn't exactly overjoyed to see that you had brought me there."

"True, but he's a very busy man, and he has gotten me this far. He knows what he's doing. You know how long it took us to get pregnant. We'd been to all those other specialists off base. He's the only doctor that has really helped us."

"I know, sweetie, but I just think that maybe you should get a second opinion about this vitamin and mineral business. It couldn't hurt."

"And I just think you shouldn't worry so much. I'm fine, Mom. Really." I tried to be as reassuring as I could. I knew she was worried, but Dr. Stanley seemed to have everything under control; and she was right before when she said that he was the sole reason for this miracle growing inside me. I would have felt like I was betraying him by seeing another doctor. As much as I hated the shots, I was determined to let Dr. Stanley see me through.

A few days had gone by, and it was already time for my mom to go home. I was miserable all morning, wishing she didn't have to leave. It had been so nice having her there to help and just be with me. Daniel helped bring her things down to the car. We all piled in to see her off at the airport. The three of us said our farewells in front of the security check, and though I really didn't want to, I had to let her go. I sobbed ridiculously as she disappeared through security, a reaction partly hormonal but mostly because I missed her so much when we were apart. Daniel hugged me tight and let me know everything would be okay and reminded me I still had him. He drove me home and let me cry in silence all the way back. He always knew exactly what to say and when to say nothing at all.

Early the following morning, Daniel was back at work, and I was busy putting the border around the nursery walls. My mom and Daniel had done all the painting for me while she was there. I wanted to help, but they both insisted I stay away from the paint fumes.

I was trying to work out a bubble on a very stubborn corner piece when I heard the phone ring. I knew I should have ignored the phone and kept trying to smooth it out before it set, but I was pretty frustrated and welcomed the distraction. I went into my bedroom to answer the call.

"Hello," I began. The caller id read *Private Name, Private Number.*

"Mrs. Lundy?" a woman's voice questioned.

"Speaking."

"Mrs. Lundy, I'm calling about your baby." She paused.

"Oh, are you from Dr. Stanley's office?" I was confused.

"No. Mrs. Lundy, I have to warn you. Don't have this baby. You have to stop seeing Dr. Stanley, and you can't have this baby."

"Who is this?" My stomach was turning. I was an odd blend of frightened and furious.

"I can't tell you who I am. It's not safe for me. They paid me to go away. They'd kill me if they knew I was telling you. The child you're carrying isn't your own. They've done something to him... and to you. You have to find a way to terminate this pregnancy before it's too late."

"Who are you? Is this some kind of sick joke? I'm going to call the MP's if you don't stop this." I was terrified. This woman was clearly disturbed.

"Are you sure the egg they put back inside you was your own? Have you been getting the injections? Does it feel sometimes like your baby is trying to tear his way out of you?"

"I don't have to answer this. You need help."

"It's not your baby, Mrs. Lundy; it's theirs, and they'll take him from you just like they took mine from me, but when they took mine, I had only just begun to figure it out, and it was too late. I'm not even sure he was human. Babies just don't do the things my Jeremy did. They don't grow that fast, and they certainly don't..." She paused again.

They don't what? I thought to myself. I actually was interested now in hearing the rest of her crazy story.

She continued, "just don't let it get that far. By the time they come for him, it will be too late. Don't let that happen."

"Who are *they*? What are you talking about?" I couldn't believe I was actually curious to hear more of this nonsense.

"Dr. Stanley and the rest of them. They need him. He's part of a greater plan. Just please, do something before it's too late. Don't bring that baby into this world. Don't let it into your home. It's dangerous," she said desperately.

"First of all, lady, if this is a joke, it isn't funny. I don't know what you have against the military or Dr. Stanley, but maybe you should take it up with him. And I don't even know if I'm having a boy or a girl yet, and I can guarantee this is *my* baby and yes, it *is* human, so I really need you to never call here again, and please, get yourself some help."

"Oh," she said, "it's a boy. You can bet that whatever it is, it's a boy." She sounded so sure and so lucid in her story telling. I was shaking with fear.

"I'm hanging up, and if you ever call here again, I will go to the authorities!" I hung up the phone and then watched it for a moment in horror, waiting for it to ring again, but it never did. I sat in silence for what seemed like forever, in shock. My first thought was to report it, but her words kept swirling in my head, and she knew so much detail about my treatment and the horrible pains I was having that Dr. Stanley explained away so many times as cramps. What would Dr. Stanley want with my baby? And why on earth would he have implanted someone or something else's egg in my body? It was unfathomable. Was I actually considering this deranged woman's delusions as truths? Maybe I was the crazy one. No, I couldn't let her get to me. I wrote it off, thinking she probably had a bad experience with the hospital on base and was just trying to get back at them by reaching out to the patients and stirring up trouble. I took several deep breaths and went downstairs to make sure the doors and windows were locked and make myself some tea.

As soon as Daniel got home, I bombarded him with the details of my bizarre phone call. He insisted I report it, but since she never did call back, and we didn't have her phone number or name, we decided to let it go and try to get it out of our minds. I'm sure releasing it from thought was easier for my husband than it was for me. That phone call haunted me for weeks.

Every time I had a pain, I thought about the baby trying to claw its way out. Every time I saw Dr. Stanley, and he administered the injections, I wanted to question him, but I didn't. I wanted to ask him about this woman every time I went in to the office, but I didn't know where to begin without sounding crazy. Eventually, I was able to put the bad feelings and thoughts out of my head and continue to look forward to meeting our son or daughter.

Before I knew it, another six weeks had passed. I was now over six months pregnant and starting to get more and more excited. The nursery was complete, and I was beginning to receive packages from my friends and my and Daniel's families. I didn't have a traditional baby shower. There were only a few women on base that I had gotten to know, but I didn't feel very close to any of them. I felt like it would be too emotional to celebrate without my mother and sister there anyway, so instead, I registered for my baby online, and everyone was able to ship us gifts directly from the website. It was sort of bittersweet opening all the packages alone, but I appreciated everyone's sentiment.

One night, halfway into my sixth month, I woke with an intense craving again for raw meat. I knew how disgusting this was, but I just couldn't shake the urge. I looked to my right and made sure Daniel was soundly sleeping. I slid carefully out of bed and crept out the door and down the stairs. I had just been shopping that day, so I knew there was a package of fresh ground beef in the refrigerator. I swung open the fridge door and saw it there, blood red, calling to me. All second thoughts and hesitations were completely gone from my mind now. I had to have it.

I grabbed the package and ripped into the cellophane. With my right hand, I tore into the meat and shoved a huge piece in my mouth. It tasted so good. I kept repeating this until the package was nearly gone.

"Rachel, what the hell?" Daniel's voice came toward me, frightening me back to reality.

I looked at the package, nearly devoured, and saw my hand stained pink. All of a sudden I felt sick to my stomach. Why had I done this? I turned toward the sink and began heaving. Luckily, I chose the side with the garbage disposal.

"Rachel, are you okay?" Daniel continued. "What were you doing?"

I took a moment, then began to wash my hands at the sink, rinsing all the blood and chunks of meat down into the drain. I dried my hand and flipped the disposal switch. Still in disbelief, I turned toward my husband, who was standing in the doorway, completely bewildered.

"Wow, uh, I don't know," I tried to explain, "I just got this craving…"

"For meat? And you couldn't wait to cook it?" Daniel was completely grossed out.

"Yeah, I know. I don't know what came over me. I just had to have it."

"That's not normal, Rach." Daniel crossed over to me, handing me a paper towel and motioning toward my face. Apparently there was still some evidence of my fridge raid left on my cheek.

"Dr. Stanley said these kinds of cravings are fairly normal actually; I just never thought I would..." I looked back toward the sink to make sure it was all down. I felt so disgusting.

"Okay, well, next time, let me know, and I'll cook it for you. That's not good for you, babe." Daniel was trying to be calm and understanding, but I knew this had to look weird to him, especially knowing that before this incident, I wouldn't even touch meat unless it was super well done and didn't even have the slightest touch of pink. At restaurants, if the burger or steak wasn't charred, it was going back.

Shaken by the last few minutes, we walked slowly back up to our bedroom and got back into bed, silently. That wasn't the last time I had that craving, but it certainly was the one and only time I would satisfy it.

Another month passed, luckily without any odd occurrences. The pains had gotten much better, that or I'd become used to them, and Dr. Stanley seemed overjoyed with the baby's progress. Daniel seemed to be doing well with his work on base. Everything appeared to be on track.

My belly was quite large by this point, and I was having trouble fitting behind the steering wheel, so I scheduled my weekly appointments around Daniel so he could drive me. He preferred it anyway. He was always glad to be there, especially the weeks we did ultrasounds, and he could see the baby.

One day, after our appointment, Daniel and I decided to drive off base to do some grocery shopping. We were so elated, having just seen our baby, that we thought nothing could ruin our high.

Coming out of the store, Daniel pushed the cart as I searched my purse for his keys. For some reason, he always handed them to me, as if he would lose them in his pocket if he had held them himself. It was a silly ritual he always did when we were out together. I had all my attention inside my purse, and just as I had located them and was fishing them out, I felt someone grab my right arm.

"Mrs. Lundy," a woman's voice said quietly as she turned me around.

I was startled. Maybe I had left something behind in the store.

"Mrs. Lundy," she continued, her voice now sounded familiar, and it made me nervous. Her face looked sad and full of fear as she glanced down at my large stomach. She took her grip away from my arm and placed a hand on my belly. "It's too late now," she said woefully. I now knew, this was the woman from the phone.

"Daniel." I stopped my husband. He turned back and glared at the woman.

"Just give them the baby when he comes. Don't bring him into your house. They'll want you to, but don't do it." She looked terrified. I stepped back to distance myself from her, but she inched closer. "You have to listen to me. It's a monster. Don't bring him home."

"You need to move along before I call the police," Daniel advised her while stepping in front of me.

"Dr. Stanley needs you to care for the baby the first month, and then they'll take him from you, but by then it will be far too late. He needs your milk. Stop the injections, and do not breast feed this thing. Don't bring that monster into your house," she warned again.

"Who are you?" Daniel questioned.

"I have to go before they see me. Please, don't tell them I was here. Just listen to me. It's too late to terminate the pregnancy, but there's still time to make a wise choice. Don't bring that thing home," she whispered. Her eyes searched around and studied the parking lot. She then took off running toward the street.

I could see Daniel's first instinct was to follow her, but I touched his arm to let him know I didn't think it wise. We let her go.

"Are you okay?" He studied my face and then hugged me tightly. He pulled out his cell phone and called 911. Since we weren't on base, we had to report it to the police first.

We still didn't know who she was. All we knew was what she looked like and that this was the second time she had harassed me. The police took our report but told us what we already knew. Since we didn't know her name or have any information regarding this person, there was really nothing they could do.

When we got home, Daniel decided to also contact the military police just in case this woman tried to contact us at home again. They weren't able to do anything either, but Daniel felt a little better having had reported it.

Daniel also thought it best to call Dr. Stanley. This woman had an obvious vendetta against him. Dr. Stanley immediately knew who Daniel was describing. He told Daniel that she was a patient of his and that, unfortunately, her pregnancy ended with a miscarriage shortly after she'd received news that her husband, a Private First Class, was killed overseas. He said that after her traumatic loss, she began experiencing these paranoid delusions, and he advised her to seek counseling. He explained that she seemed to be getting better, but that she had moved off base about a year before and was obviously experiencing some sort of PTSD relapse. Dr. Stanley never did offer her name, but he did tell Daniel that he would call the MP's himself to add to the report in case the woman hassled us again. Daniel thanked the doctor, relayed the story to me, and we decided to try once again to put it out of our minds.

I felt sorry for the poor woman. I couldn't imagine, experiencing my first pregnancy while my husband was fighting in another country. Although, in our case, because of our fertility issues, it would have never happened that way, and for that I felt extremely lucky. My Daniel had toured twice, and granted, while it wasn't impossible that he would be called out again, he was, for that time being, firmly planted right there on base. Him being stationed in the United States as a Corporal was one of the reasons we could even consider fertility treatments. Had he been overseas, it wouldn't have been an option. I knew how blessed I was, but this poor woman lost her husband and her baby within a month of each other. My heart swelled with sadness for her situation, and my pity completely replaced my fear that I had first experienced before I had been made aware of her history.

Weeks went by without a visit or a phone call from the disillusioned woman. Things were seemingly back to normal. Days after the last incident with her, I had signed up for Lamaze classes off base at the women's center. They were at night, which was great for Daniel. We only went to a few, but felt far more prepared for the birth. The doctor's visits were still going well, and Dr. Stanley seemed very pleased with my and the baby's progress. I asked him about the poor woman that harassed Daniel and I in the parking lot that day, and he just smiled and said that he was able to get her back into treatment, and she should be better soon.

At a little over eight months pregnant, I really couldn't wait to get the baby out. Sure, I had bonded with my child and had the warm and fuzzies, as pregnant women do, but I was also really tired of carrying around the extra weight, and I couldn't stand my now extremely swollen ankles and impossibly huge fingers. On a Saturday night, just over two weeks away from my due date, my water broke. Daniel grabbed my hospital bag and sweetly assisted me to the car. Once at the hospital, I was sent right into a delivery room. My contractions were coming very quickly and were very intense.

Dr. Stanley rushed into the room to examine me. I was in so much pain, and everything was kind of a blur. He abruptly turned to the nurse and asked her to prepare me for the OR.

"Wait, Dr. Stanley?" I yelled after him, confused, but he was already on his way out the door. He didn't even address me. As I tried to get someone to tell me what was going on, they were already putting a mask over my face. Daniel wasn't in the room at that time, and I was terrified. The last thing I remember is the nurse telling me to breathe deep and count backwards from ten, something I did not comply with, but the anesthesia took effect all the same.

I woke hours later inside a very small hospital room. I felt pressure on my hand, and looked over to see Daniel holding it. He jumped up as soon as he saw me move.

"Are you alright, Rach?" he started.

"The baby?" I asked. "Where's the baby?"

"He's okay. He's with the nurses. He's beautiful, Rach, just beautiful." He squeezed my hand in reassurance.

"He?" I was excited to hear it was a boy. "I want to see him."

"They'll bring him in when you're ready. How are you feeling?"

"I'm fine." I smiled at my husband. "I just want to see him."

Daniel got up to find the nurse and our son. He returned with a nurse holding our baby with Dr. Stanley close behind.

"Hello. Meet your baby boy," Dr. Stanley said as he slowly closed the door behind them. He noticed my confused glare and took the cue. "As you are aware, Rachel, there were some complications during labor. We had to perform a C-section. I know it wasn't part of your original birthing plan, but the baby was turned backwards, and we didn't have much time. Fortunately, the surgery went very smoothly, and he is just fine. You'll be in pain for quite some time, but the incision line should heal within four to five weeks, and if you keep the ointment on it, it will be barely noticeable. I'll get you some to take home."

"Okay." I was still furious with how it happened, but if he was saying there was no time, then I had to accept that he did what he had to do. I turned my attention to my baby boy. The nurse came to my bedside to hand him to me. He was the most perfect creature I had ever seen. Tears strolled down my face as I looked at the boy we had created. "Hello, Tucker." It just came out. I guess it was destined to be his name all along, despite my constant rejection of the idea.

"Really?" Daniel stepped over. "Thank you," he said as he wiped a tear from his own face. Tucker was his grandfather's name. "Hey there, Tuck." He let the baby latch his tiny hand onto his finger. This could not have been a more perfect moment.

"Now," Dr. Stanley cut in, "when you are ready, the nurse will show you the proper way to breast feed. This is extremely important for Tucker and for you. You must do it for the first few days. It's imperative to his development."

"Alright," I replied. He had caught me off guard, but he was right. I had intended on breastfeeding. "Thank you, Dr. Stanley. Thank you for everything."

"Sure," he said, "I will let you have your time. Please let me know if you need anything." He smiled, turned, and left the room.

A few days later, I was ready to go home. Daniel, Tucker, and I were on our way to beginning our new lives together.

When we got back to the house, the first thing I wanted to do was call my mother. I wasn't able to dial out when we were at the hospital, and for some reason, neither of our cell phones were working. The internet was also down, and we couldn't get it straightened out. My mom still had no idea I'd had Tucker. Daniel took baby Tuck upstairs, and I waddled to the phone in the kitchen. When I picked it up, there was no dial tone. I still wasn't able to call her and share the news. In frustration I threw the phone and broke into tears.

Once Daniel had put the baby safely in his crib, he came back downstairs to console me.

"It's okay," he said. "I'll drive into town tomorrow and see if we can get someone out here to check the lines." He held me close until the tears subsided.

That night, I was exceptionally tired. The baby, however, was being very quiet. I checked in on him every five minutes to make sure he was alright and to watch him sleep. He did wake in the evening, and I was able to feed him then. This feeding was a little different than the feedings I'd given the days before. He seemed hungrier than usual, and it seemed he bit me. I was startled when this happened, but I just switched sides and decided it was probably just a tear.

Finally, around three, Daniel convinced me to go to bed. I fell asleep hard, and was deep into the sleep cycle when a loud crash ripped me away from dreamland. I looked around the room with hazy eyes. I wasn't sure I'd really heard the noise until Daniel started to scream out. I'd never heard him yell this way before. He was being attacked. My first instinct was to call the MPs. I reached for the phone on the nightstand, but it was dead. I then reached inside the nightstand drawer. Daniel had always kept a gun in there; a gun that I couldn't find now that I actually needed it.

Daniel made one more loud scream, and then I heard a thump in the kitchen. I had to get the baby.

Fear created a lump in my abdomen. My stomach was already tight and sore from the surgery, but it now felt very heavy. I pulled myself from my bed and carefully crept toward the bedroom door. I swung around the door jamb and into the nursery next door. I shuffled to the crib and reached my arms in for Tucker, but I felt nothing. He wasn't there.

All I could think was that my family was in danger, and I had to get to them. I tip toed to the stairs and quietly stepped down. I instinctively held my stomach where the incision was. I wasn't really aware of it at the time, but it was throbbing. I reached the bottom of the staircase, and that's when I saw the first bit of blood. There was a small pool of blood on the hardwood floor of the entryway. I was terrified. For a brief moment I contemplated getting myself back up the stairs. I wasn't sure I could handle finding out who the blood belonged to. I continued on and swiftly turned the corner from the entry into the living room.

My heart stopped, and I couldn't take in air. I felt the blood in my veins stop flowing as all my muscles froze up and my skin went numb. All of a sudden a deep rage and terror welled up inside, and from the bottom of my stomach came a scream so loud, a scream so unfamiliar, that I wasn't even sure I'd really let it out.

There, on the floor, was my son, laying on top of my husband. Daniel was covered in blood and not moving. Tucker sat up. He sat up as if he were already months old. I knew this was impossible. I couldn't process what I was seeing. He turned to me, face covered in blood, and he opened his mouth. I saw tiny jagged teeth. Newborn babies don't have teeth. Infants don't sit up. This was impossible. I had to be asleep. This had to be a nightmare. He opened his eyes, and he looked right at me. I wanted to run to

Daniel, I wanted to run out the door and keep running, but at the same time, I also had this urge to just scoop Tucker up and hold him close. I didn't know what to do. My muscles remained frozen.

The baby climbed down from Daniel and began crawling in my direction. I knew he shouldn't be crawling. None of this could be real. All I could do, though, was watch in disbelief and horror. My face was hot. It felt like it was on fire. I could feel myself crying. Each tear felt like ice as it went down my burning skin. The baby kept coming and was now at my leg.

He sat and looked up at me like he wanted me to pick him up. I had to. There wasn't anything else I could do. So I did. I reached down for this monster, for my baby. He curled up in my arms. He cooed as if he were cozy and happy, and then, he fell asleep. I closed my eyes and tried to decide what to feel, what to think, what to do. I rocked Tucker as he slept, and I went to Daniel's side. I knelt down and saw that he was definitely gone. Grief took over my body. This was supposed to be the best time of our lives. This was supposed to be our dream realized.

Just as the reality of this hellish situation began to wash over me, I heard a loud commotion outside. I saw the lights from the MP vehicles. I wanted to run to the door and cry out for help, but at the same time, I felt that I had to protect my son.

As the possibilities of what might happen next danced around my head, the front door burst open.

I saw several men in protective gear flood my home. I would have been taken aback by this, but it seemed nothing could shock me now, or so I thought.

"Phase one complete, Doctor," one of the men said. "Subject 475-A is ready for retrieval."

"Thank you." Dr. Stanley appeared from around the corner. "Please apprehend the subject."

A solider stepped forward with a small cage.

"What?" I stepped back, confused. "What are you doing? What's going on?"

"Mrs. Lundy," Dr. Stanley started, "please, give the gentleman the baby."

"No! Tell me what is going on! What is wrong with Tucker?"

"Tucker," Dr. Stanley explained, "is a very valuable weapon. The initial testing phase is complete. Your milk is no longer needed, and therefore, you are no longer of use to this experiment. We must remove the test subject from your home before he begins to expand."

"Expand? Test? What are you talking about? This is my baby!"

"No, Mrs. Lundy. I'm sorry; he's not." Dr. Stanley was feigning compassion. "We implanted an embryo, but not of your DNA. Not Daniel's either. I'm very sorry to tell you this, but that child is not yours; you were just the vessel we used to grow him in. He feels a special bond for you because he knows what you've done for him. They all feel close to their incubators. In the next couple days, as he grows, he will forget you, but please, don't feel bad; you've done your country a great service. Someday Subject 475-A, I mean Tucker, and those like him, will lead an army. They will be invincible. Imagine a legion of ruthless killers. An army programmed from birth for one thing and one thing only, destruction. No emotions, no ties, no real sense of right or wrong; just pure, organized killing machines. It's beautiful, and you helped. You can feel good knowing that you've done your part to protect this great nation. Daniel too. He, in fact, was a great part of what we've been working on. We have several warfare projects going on in that hangar. He didn't know about this one in particular, but he sure will be missed by his own team."

My eyes weighed heavy. I couldn't fully grasp what was happening. My grip on Tucker grew softer. The soldier seized his opportunity to take the baby from me and put him in his carrier. I looked back at my husband's lifeless body.

"Don't worry, Rachel. Daniel will have died a hero. He is a hero. Without him having let 475-A do what he needed to do, this wouldn't be possible. The first kill is of great importance in their development. They've been genetically engineered. The injections were part of the modification process. See, the remnants of the drugs we've been giving you were left over in your milk. Once the subject is weaned off the high dosage he's been receiving in the womb, he is able to begin developing into the machine he needs to be. His first kill always takes place by the fourth day; you can almost set a timer to it. This first kill is instinctive, and it is very important. It really shapes the kind of soldier they eventually grow into over the next few years."

"A few years?" I was stunned.

"Yes, Rachel. Within a matter of three or four short years, Tucker here will be a fully grown soldier, ready for war. It's glorious. They're doing this all over the country. We're almost ready. We hit a few bumps in the road, had a few experiments gone awry. We've had some trouble with a mutation that has occurred in some cases. Those experiments had to be exterminated, but 475-A here is just perfect. So far, so good." He looked into the cage pleased with his project.

"That woman; she tried to warn me," I said as I tried to catch my breath.

"Oh, yes. Mrs. Farmer. Well, she had a very unfortunate accident just recently. I don't think you'll be hearing from her again." Dr. Stanley smirked. "That brings me to your options. Now we're not really big on threats here, but let's face it, there's nothing like a little fear to spark incentive. So here's what we can do, you can join your husband and baby in the fatal car accident they're about to have on the way back from the hospital, or you can still be in the hospital recovering when you hear the terrible news, and you can walk away from this whole thing a little richer. Did we tell you that as of midnight tonight Daniel's accidental life insurance policy was worth over three million dollars? That's pretty substantial. Now, if you choose door number two, and we let you walk, you are to never speak of this experiment or what happened here tonight. We have eyes and ears everywhere, and I do mean everywhere. If we find out you've been giving away our secrets, we will have no choice but to remove you as well."

The idea of going on without Daniel was unbearable. I couldn't imagine a life without him. Either way, he was gone. If I went along with their plan, I'd have to lie. I'd have to tell my mom my family died in a car crash. How could I do that? The options swirled around my head. I knew I wasn't leaving there until I agreed to one or the other. If I chose to walk, I might be able to find some way to exact revenge in the future. That seemed like my only real option, my only chance of survival.

"Okay," I looked into the small grates on the cage at Tucker's blood stained face and said goodbye. He looked back and seemed to acknowledge the sentiment. He didn't cry. He didn't seem phased at all. I didn't turn back to Daniel. I didn't want to see him like that again. "Alright, Doctor. I'll do it. I'll take the money."

"That's my girl." Pleased with my calm decision making, Dr. Stanley escorted me quietly to the kitchen, where I was explained all the details of the supposed death of my son and husband. Dr. Stanley advised he would be contacting my mother. He'd make arrangements for her to come out and help me gather some essentials. I was to then leave the base and never look back.

That's what I did, or so it seemed. I didn't speak of what had really happened, but I didn't forget either. No one ever saw anything in the press about these genetically engineered soldiers, but *I* knew they were still being raised. I knew they were out there. I didn't have any kind of plan for revenge against the base or the soldiers that were involved in what happened to us. Dr. Stanley, on the other hand, I'm about to commence phase one.

CAMPFIRE TALES

The group settled in around the campfire. The six of them had been friends since high school. Now, nearing their thirties, they felt it especially important to cling to old tradition and go on this yearly, group camping trip. Nick and Shelly were the Momma and Daddy Bear of the group. They'd been together since freshman year of high school. Nick was the typical golden boy, football hero, and Shelly was always at every game to cheer him on in her pep squad uniform. They were prom king and queen senior year, and they of course went on to the same college. After college, Nick and Shelly went into business with Shelly's father and later became proud partners in a very large furniture chain. Of the six, Shelly and Nick were always seen as the most successful and most with it. None of the others really understood how they'd managed to keep their relationship so solid all those years, but they didn't question it out loud because they knew their own deep seeded jealousy would show.

Across from Nick and Shelly sat Rob and Jennifer. Rob and Jennifer dated in high school as well, but once Rob realized he might actually prefer males, he and Jennifer split up. The two became the best of friends and eventually ended up roommates. They still lived together, and the rest of the circle sometimes found their connection annoying. They were inseparable.

Everything he did, she did, and everything she did, he did. It got to the point where they had their own kind of secret language. They'd just look at each other, make some sort of noise, or say an insignificant word, and they'd start cracking up or nod to each other in agreement as if there was an actual thought communicated between their brains by an invisible messenger. This special bond left the others feeling left out at times and completely annoyed at others; but just as Nick and Shelly were accepted as one entity, so were Rob and Jennifer.

Then there was Tate and Rae. Tate was the group comedian. He was always quick with the jokes, and he had this way of making light of absolutely any situation. They all loved him to death, but they feared that his stand-up routine was just a front to mask his fear of settling down and finding someone to share his life with. He insisted he was just fine being single. Though he hadn't had a serious relationship to speak of in his entire life, he was quite the ladies' man. He was a classic serial dater. Tate was not a fan of commitment, and he didn't share his friends' desire to couple up and procreate. Rae, however, was much different. She was the most virtuous of the clan. She received straight A's in school, and while her friends were out experimenting with alcohol and sex, she was always at home studying and waiting for the drunken phone calls in which her friends were always begging for rides home. She was married to a man named Michael, who had a similarly tepid approach to life. The two of them threw the occasional dinner party and made time each month for bingo at the community center. The group called them Mr. and Mrs. Old Fart. Michael was always invited to go on the camping excursions, but he never accepted the invitations. He claimed he wanted Rae to have the time to bond with her friends, but in reality, the idea of being out in the woods, away from the comforts of home, terrified him.

They all sat around the fire, each with a beer in hand, even Rae. The six friends reflected on their long day of fishing, and they lamented that none of them were able to catch anything.

"Okay, okay. Enough about the stupid fish. Who here wants to tell ghost stories?" Nick asked.

"Nick," Rob replied, "we always come up here and tell the same old, tired stories. I really don't want to hear about the guy with a hook for a hand again or that lame ass story about the babysitter and the stalker guy or whatever."

"Okay. Fair enough." Nick took a sip from his bottle as he contemplated his next move. "Okay!" he announced as his face lit up with excitement. "I think I have a new one. I can guarantee you haven't heard it before."

The group sneered at the idea.

"Come on, honey," Shelly pleaded, "let's just bust out the marshmallows or something."

"Uh oh," Tate said from across the dancing flames, "it sounds like somebody's a little scared."

"Shut up!" Shelly yelled playfully. "I'm not scared of silly little ghost stories."

"This isn't silly, Shelly," her husband said, "it really happened."

Shelly pinched him in the arm and giggled. She flashed him a defeated sideways glance and then exhaled and motioned to let him know she wouldn't fight him again if he really wanted to continue.

"No. That's alright. If Shells here is scared of a little bitty story, we don't have to go on," Nick jested.

"Story! Story!" Tate chanted, pumping his fist in the air. He grabbed Rae's hand and waved it in the air in unison with his other fist. She laughed and began chanting too.

Within seconds, Rob and Jennifer followed and the four of them repeated the word and shook their fists with glee.

"Story! Story! Story! Story!" the four called out.

"Okay!" Nick threw his free hand up in the air and then took a sip of his beer from the other. "Okay, fine. I'll tell the story. Just be warned... it's pretty scary, and like I said, it could happen."

"I thought you said it already did happen!" Jennifer shouted, disappointed. "Bogus!"

"Did happen; Could happen... same thing," Nick retorted, laughing.

"Alright." Jennifer shot a disapproving look his way that quickly turned into a smile, followed by a laugh. "Continue, Sir Nick, with your fabulous story."

"Okay," Nick said. He cleared his throat and started stretching his arms. The group watched as he put his beer down and proceeded to crack his knuckles and then his neck.

"Oh, come on!" Tate shouted. The friends all laughed.

"Okay. Sorry. I had to get prepared. This is serious business you know?" Nick's face cracked into a smile. He picked up his beer bottle, took a swig, and continued. "It was a warm June night, a lot like this one. The stars were shining, and the moon was watching from above as six friends sat around a campfire, much like that one." He pointed toward the fire pit.

"Ahhh man!" Tate swatted his hand in disapproval.

"No, no," Nick defended himself as the circle hissed at him. "Just wait. This is for real. Let's see... there were six of them..." He looked around the circle, studying the faces of his friends. "There was Kelly," he said as he looked at his wife. "There was Rick," he nodded to himself then moved to the right, "Nate, Mae, Bob, and..." He looked at Jennifer. He had stumped himself. "Lennifer."

"Okay, you jackass. Lennifer is not a name, and this is not going to be a good story," Jennifer claimed, again very disappointed.

"Okay. Okay. I'm sorry. We'll call her Francine." He giggled to himself.

"Francine?" Jennifer asked. "You're random."

"Hey!" Nick said, "may I please finish my story, Francine? I mean, Jennifer?"

"Okay. Sure." She sipped her beer and let Nick continue.

"Okay. No more interruptions guys." Nick held his hands up to emphasize the seriousness of his request. They all nodded in agreement to let him go on.

"Alright then," Nick continued. "There was Kelly, Vic...."

"Rick," Shelly corrected him.

"Right, Rick. Thank you, baby," he said, glancing toward his wife. "There was Kelly, Rick, Nate, Mae, Bob and Francine. The six of them sat around their campfire drinking beer and talking about the good old days. They reminisced about how great high school was, or in Nate's case, how terrible it was, and how they were so glad to still have such a strong bond. They had taken the same camping trip since their senior year, and they always had the best time. Little did they know, this camping trip would be different. This camping trip would be their last..." Nick lingered on his final word for dramatic effect.

"Dun, Dun, DUUNNN!!!!" Tate added.

"Thank you, Tate," Nick offered. "You see," he went on, "there was a secret in their circle. It was something none of the others would believe, and it was that something that would soon tear them all apart."

The campers all glanced around at each other, searching each other's faces. They didn't know if Nick was really about to reveal something. They laughed nervously, but were anticipating something real.

"Oh my god!" Tate yelled out. "You two are thinking of spawning!" He pointed at Shelly and Nick. "Aw, man! This sucks! What a crappy way to tell us, man."

"What?" Shelly fired back. "No." She looked to her husband.

Nick laughed as he replied, "no, dude. Don't worry. Shelly and I aren't having kids any time soon."

"Oh, thank God!" Tate exhaled with relief. " 'Cause you know, first it's *oh don't worry, we can get a sitter*, but then it's like, *oh we can't go out tonight, little Darlene has a ballet recital, and Nick Jr. needs me to help him with his science project.*" Tate shivered at the thought and shook out his hands as if trying to cleanse himself of the image.

"Good to know how you feel, man," Nick said. "Now, can I continue?"

"Yeah. Sorry. You scared me, bro. Ah, see, your story telling is very effective."

"I guess it is." Nick laughed at his friend. "Moving on." Nick took a deep breath in and continued with his story. "As I was saying... there was a secret. One person in the circle was hiding something from the rest. Something dark. Something evil."

They all laughed and looked around in relief. They were sure Nick was obviously joking, and no one was really hiding anything.

Confident he had them all at ease and intrigued, Nick went on.

"They had been friends for many years. They knew each other's deepest darkest secrets. There was nothing the six friends didn't know about one another; nothing except the most important secret of all. Their dearest most beloved pal Rick was keeping his greatest desires under lock and key, and tonight, they would finally be let free."

"I knew it!" Tate cut in again. "You have a thing for Rob!"

They all laughed heartily.

"Uh, no thank you. No offense, but he is so not my type," Rob volunteered.

"Very funny guys. No, I do not have a thing for Rob." Nick patted Shelly's hand in playful reassurance. "Rick doesn't have a thing for Bob either."

"Aw. Too bad," Jennifer offered up as she nudged her roommate.

"Back to the story," Nick demanded with frustration.

The crowd silenced as if being scolded by a grade school teacher. They glanced around, throwing little smiles at each other like bratty children in trouble.

"Anyway," Nick began, "Rick wasn't who they all thought he was. Rick didn't enjoy all the things his friends did, and in fact, Rick didn't even really enjoy his friends. He hated them. He despised each and every one of them, all for a different reason, but the hate for each was all the same."

Glances between the friends were once again exchanged around the fire. They all shrugged at each other and tried to smile, hoping this wasn't actually leading into something hurtful.

"He hated them," Nick continued. "He couldn't stand Nate and his constant wise cracks. He hated the way Nate always had something sarcastic to say and the way he was always butting in." His eyes flashed to Tate.

"I dunno, man. I think everybody loves a comedian," Tate joked.

Nick kept going, un-phased. His eyes leapt again to a new person. He skipped Rae and focused his stare on Rob and Jennifer.

"Bob and Francine," Nick said, "gay Bob and sad, desperate, will always be alone Francine. Those two really made Rick sick to his stomach. He couldn't stand the way they used each other to hide from the rest of the world. They were whores. Each brining home different men all the time but saving true commitment for only each other. He wanted to shake them and say *GET A BOYFRIEND! The both of you!* Rick saw that they were both so afraid to grow up and branch out. He hated that they'd morphed into practically the same person. They were a hideous, combined being. Sure they had each other, but how sad that they'd always really be so alone. Sad, pathetic whores."

"Hey, man!" Rob jumped to his feet. "This is getting a little personal, don't you think? Maybe you should just cool it before one of us gets really pissed off."

"He's just joking," Shelly defended Nick nervously. "Right, honey? Maybe you should stop."

"No, Shells. I'm just getting started," he said robotically as he turned to her. "Sweet, beautiful Kelly. She was the prom queen and head cheerleader, and that's pretty much how everyone still saw her. She would never be anything but a perfect, perky, little cheer squad victim. She had to have the perfect body, the perfect house, the perfect husband, and the perfect every damn thing else. It drove Rick insane having to pretend all the time. He was forced to pretend that he fit so tidily into this tiny little box of flawlessness that Kelly had created for him. Since they were kids, it was always, do this, do that, act this way, and dress that way. He could no longer stomach the restrictions, and he could no longer bear the weight of the expectations."

"That is not funny, Nick!" Shelly yelled. "Stop it now!" She grabbed at his sleeve, but he pulled away.

"Then," he said, "there was Mae, sweet little Mae. Everyone loved Mae; everyone except for Rick that is. Rick used to love Mae. He used to love Mae with all his heart. No one knew that. No one knew about the two of them. They only slept together once in college. To him it meant everything, but for her it was different. She claimed she felt guilty for betraying her best friend Kelly. Rick didn't love Kelly. He told Mae that he'd leave Kelly for her in a heartbeat. She maintained that she didn't want to upset Kelly and the rest of their precious little group. He tried his best to convince her that they should be together, but she wouldn't budge. Her values were too high. Her morals were too strong. Morals!" Nick snorted and stood up as he addressed Rae. "What kind of girl sleeps with her best friend's boyfriend and goes on as if it never happened? I'll tell you what kind... the whorish, lying, devoid of morals, bitch kind. That's who!"

Rae started crying and sobbing uncontrollably. Tate put his arm around her, bewildered by the scene that had just unfolded.

"Oh," Nick said in revelation, "I guess there were two secrets then. Woops."

"Is this true?" Shelly stood up and started grabbing at her husband's shirt. "What is this?" she asked, tears welling up in her eyes. "Is it true?" she demanded.

"Wait," Nick said calmly, "I'm not done telling my story. So there they were," he continued with no inflection, "sitting around the campfire. They were all having a great time. Each was wrapped up in their own sad little universe when Rick decided to finally reveal himself. *None of you know who I am!* he said. *And none of you know what you have turned me into.* Just as he finished his last word, he pulled out a large, shiny axe, wait no, a chainsaw. He had been hiding a chainsaw underneath a blanket behind the log he and Kelly were sitting on. It looked kind of like this one." Nick bent over the log he and Shelly had been resting on and grabbed up a sixteen inch chainsaw from beneath a towel. None of his friends had seen him place it there. Shock and horror spread across their faces. Silence moved through them. All that could be heard was the crackling of the fire.

"Wait guys," Nick cut through the quiet. "It gets better. Rick pulled the cord on his chainsaw, igniting a fire within himself. His friends all scrambled as he went around the circle, but none of them were able to get away. He killed each and every one of them. They'd held him down for years, making him less and less of a man, until one day, a monster took over. These people were the reason he had spent the last fourteen years of his life in complete misery. That night, Nick got his revenge."

"You mean Rick," Shelly timidly corrected through her tears.

"No, baby. I mean Nick."

With that, Nick placed the chainsaw on the log surface for stability. He pushed the chain brake forward and then pulled the starter rope. The roar of the saw made everyone jump. Shelly turned to run, but it was too late. The revolving chain cut into her, and she fell to the ground. Nick then turned toward Rae and Tate, who were scrambling to get over the lawn chairs they were using. Nick buzzed Tate's leg. The wound was great enough to stop him where he was. He yelled out for Rae to run, and she headed for the trees.

Rob and Jennifer had also gone toward the woods, but Nick being the avid jock he was, caught up to them quickly, killing them both with little effort. He then went off looking for his love.

"Rae!" he called out over the rattling of the chainsaw. "Rae! Where are you?"

He cut the engine and listened to the woods. He heard a crackling sound to his left but was then drawn to his right. He could hear a faint sobbing sound. Once Rae got started crying, she'd usually end up hyperventilating, and it was nearly impossible to get her to stop. He followed the sound of her cries to a dark tree. She was just on the other side of it.

"Rae," Nick said in a consoling voice, "I really didn't want it to come to this. I just wanted to be with you. All I've ever wanted was to be with you; just me and you. All those disgusting people were constant reminders that you and I weren't together. They're the reason we couldn't make it work. Them!" Nick said angrily. "And you let them get in the way! You let them!"

He once again started up his weapon and leapt around the tree to find his beloved. She didn't fight him. She looked into his eyes as he held the chainsaw up to her.

"I'm sorry," she said under her breath.

Nick didn't hear it, but he saw it. He knew she meant it too. He took a breath in as he acknowledge her apology and then followed through with the blade.

Once Rae had taken her last breath, Nick went back to the campsite to find his dear friend Tate, but Tate was gone. The SUV they'd driven up in together was still there. Nick patted the outside of his front pocket and heard a jingle. Tate wasn't going to get very far.

Nick could see a trail of blood and swept dirt, where Tate was obviously dragging his wounded leg. He knew it would be easy to find him and very easy to catch him, but he also knew that Tate wouldn't survive the night, and he decided to let him go and fight it out for himself in the wilderness.

"And they say that sometimes at night you can still smell the gasoline from the chainsaw. Some people say that you can even hear it," a giddy teenager told her four girlfriends as they huddled around their campfire. "It happened right here, in this very campground."

"Yeah right," another girl scoffed.

"No, it really happened," the storyteller went on. "They never found that Nick guy, and they say he's still out here, wandering the woods."

"Well," said the skeptic, "what happened to Tate?"

"Oh yeah! So gross! When the rangers came upon this camp three days later, they found pieces of him over there behind those trees. He had been torn apart by a grizzly bear!"

The group of girls sighed in disgust. They looked around the fire, trying to size up each other's fear. They were all terrified but were trying desperately not to let it show.

"True story!" the girl continued. "My sister's best friend's brother said he saw it on the news. Anyway... sleep tight!"

LUCY

Growing up, there is nothing quite as painful as the countdown to summer break. As a boy, I found school especially tedious. Why would anyone want to be locked up in a room learning about dead people and their discoveries hundreds of years ago, when you could be outside soaking up the sun? Sure you have the buffers that make school slightly more bearable. There's the three day weekends; thank God for dead presidents; and then, of course, you have your winter break and spring break, which, don't get me wrong, are awesome, but nothing satisfies the itch quite like summer vacation. The first day of school is pure torture, but you get used to it after a bit. You tread along, knowing that eventually you will be released from your prison. Then, the last week of school finally arrives, and it is the absolute worst. The anticipation builds and builds, and paying attention in class is no longer a reasonable request. Good thing, when I was a kid, we had cool teachers in middle school that understood our woe. The last week at least was always made fun by our leaders. They would fill the last days with crafts and games. They knew better than to try and harness our daydreaming minds.

The summer of 1994 was especially memorable. I had just turned twelve and was about to embark on the most exciting summer of all time. I was becoming a man. Fifth grade is fine and dandy, but sixth grade, well you're almost an adult. Too old for kiddy stuff, but still young enough to enjoy the simple pleasures, like tree swings and playing stick ball with your friends. Lucky for me, I still found girls slightly irritating, so most of my time was spent on more productive things, like climbing trees and taking Lucy down to the creek on explorative missions.

Lucy was the best friend I'd ever had. I know I said I didn't like girls much, but she was different, mostly because she was a dog. She wasn't just any dog though; she was special. She really knew me and understood me better than any of my friends. My dock-tailed Doberman mix and I were inseparable. We went everywhere together. It was Lucy and Simon against the world. She was the first one to greet me every morning and the protector at my feet during the night.

Every morning that I had to go to school, I felt so guilty leaving my best friend at home alone. She always looked so sad when I put that book bag on my shoulder, and she was always so excited when I got home. Lucy always seemed eager for summer too. She knew it meant more time to explore and hang out.

Finally it had come. The first day of three glorious months of freedom. I woke that first morning and shot out of bed. Lucy tried to wait patiently for me to get dressed, but she was dancing across the floor in anticipation. I threw on whatever from the floor looked clean enough, laced up my sneakers, and headed for the door.

"What do you and Lucy have planned for today?" my mother asked as we made our way through the kitchen.

"I dunno," I said, letting my words run together. "Creek probably."

"Okay. Do you want some breakfast before you go?"

"No, thanks." I motioned for Lucy to follow me, and we leapt out the screen door into the warm, summer air.

"Wait!"

I turned to see my mother hanging out the screen door with an offering in a paper bag. She knew I'd be out all day, so she packed me a lunch. I, of course, never thought of things like that until I was already out and about. Growing up in the peaceful rural town I did, left my parents little to worry about. They knew it was pretty safe for me to be creek side all day as long as I didn't try to catch a poisonous snake or make friends with a rabid raccoon.

"Thanks, Mom!" I exclaimed giddily. I grabbed the lunch sack and turned back toward our path.

"Be careful down there!" my mother called after us. "Watch for snakes!"

I waved, but I didn't say anything in response. I was too intent on getting us into the trees just beyond our back fence and down to the creek that lay just below. The creek was only an eight minute walk from the house. My parents worried about flooding in the rainy season, but they never did experience a problem in all the years they lived there. Somehow, the creek always maintained a docile level.

Once we reached the water, Lucy always had to jump into the middle and explore. She was knee deep searching for something to capture. Once, she found a fish that had managed to swim up from the hatchery. They usually didn't make it that far, or even try, but one brave little fish made the journey, and Lucy was there to meet him. Every time since, she looked and looked, even though she never again found one.

"Lucy, there ain't no fish in there!" I called out, but she ignored me and kept on with the hunt.

I chuckled as she kept at it. I turned away for a moment and moved a couple steps toward our fort. Lucy and I had built it two years before. Well, I built it, and she supervised. My dad had given me a couple large metal sheets and instructed me on the proper construction of shelter forts. I insisted I could do it on my own and went down and built a fairly sturdy shelter against a large tree trunk with metal walls and a tree branch roof. It held up through all the weather, likely because it was tied down and protected by all the surrounding trees. My craftsmanship received a thumbs up when my dad came down to inspect the project upon completion. He said it was safe enough for us to play in, and so we did. Of course as the years passed by, I visited the fort less and less and eventually just stopped all together, but I'd bet it's still down there. It was certainly there and definitely occupied more often than not during the summer days of '94. Lucy and I played for hours down there in our little hideaway. I'd sit under the branches as sun leaked through the roof, and I'd toss rocks in the water for Lucy to chase. She never retrieved the rocks, but she sure liked to follow them in. That's what we did that day. We just sat, soaking up the nature around us. I threw rocks, and Lucy chased them. All seemed right with the world.

After nearly a whole day of playing creek side, we made the trek back home. As I said, it was only eight minutes, but somehow the coming home part seemed longer. We never really wanted to go home, but I had to check in with my mom once she got home from work.

"Well," she said as we came in from the back door into the kitchen, "did you two have fun?"

"Yep." For some reason, back then, I always kept it short.

"Aah!" she exclaimed. "That dog is soaking wet! Outside!" She motioned for Lucy to go back out. "Go on! Out!"

Lucy pouted and threw herself in reverse. What was left of her little tail shimmied back and forth.

"Mom, she's not that bad." I came quickly to my friend's defense.

"Simon Andrew," she said, using my first and middle name; never a good thing. "You know you can't bring her in here after she's been playing in the creek. I just did the floors. She can come in when she's dry."

"Okay," I said, annoyed.

"Wash up. Your dad will be home soon, and dinner's almost ready."

I headed off to clean up. Thoughts of our adventure swirled around my head. I couldn't wait to get up and do it again the next day.

Later that night, Lucy was allowed back in the house, and we stayed up watching a comedy on TV with my mom and dad. I was an only child, so bed time was never a huge production for my parents. I rarely protested. They were pretty lenient and usually let me stay up until ten, and since most of the other kids I knew had to be in their beds by nine, I always felt special, like I was getting away with something.

At ten o'clock, I let Lucy out one more time so she could go to the bathroom, and when she came back in, we went off to bed. She waited politely, as she did every night, for me to get in bed first. Once I was nestled in the covers, she jumped up and took her place at my feet.

"Night, Lucy," I said. She lifted her head in response and then put it back down and closed her eyes.

The excitement from the day must have worn me out. I fell asleep quickly. I was startled awake by a tug at the bottom of my comforter. I jumped and looked down to see Lucy standing on the floor, tugging at my covers.

"Hey, you need to go out?" I asked my friend. She whimpered in desperation. I looked at the clock next to me which read 3:01, and I sighed a little with slight, groggy eyed protest. "Okay. Come on girl." I got up and headed for the door.

I let Lucy out and waited by the front door. While waiting, I had shut the door so as not to let the summer bugs in. We had a screen door, but there were a couple holes in it that needed patching, and the smaller creepy crawlies somehow always managed to find their way in.

I usually could hear Lucy's feet coming up the steps before she reached the door, so I always knew when to let her in. I posted myself up against the door jamb and closed my tired eyes. I was soon startled by a scratching at the door. I figured it was Lucy; I must have not heard her on the steps.

I swung open the main door, revealing the screen, and I saw Lucy standing there on the porch. Her fur looked slimy and matted down on one side, like she had been sweating or had gotten hit by the sprinkler, but the sprinklers weren't on, and dogs don't sweat that way.

"You okay, Lucy?"

She didn't look up at me; she kept her head down toward the ground.

"Hey, girl, what's wrong?"

I went to open the screen but was stopped short when her head snapped up quickly, and she sharply cocked it to the left. Something seemed very different about her. As I studied her face, I realized it wasn't Lucy. I froze in horror as the dog's face slowly contorted into a twisted smile. I wanted to call out for my dad, but my mouth couldn't get the words out. I tried and tried, but my voice was muted.

"Aren't you going to invite me in?" the thing snarled. It spoke! I couldn't believe what I was seeing and hearing. It's voice was deep and rough, and there was a slight gurgle in between the drawn out words. "Well?" it hissed.

"No!" I finally got my voice back. "Lucy! Where's Lucy?" I demanded from the creature.

"I'm Lucy. Come on, kid, let me in." I searched the darkness behind this demon dog, hoping and praying I would see my sidekick out there, but all I saw was black. I held the handle of the screen door tight, fearing that it might try to come in on its own. The lock didn't work anymore, so all I could do was hold it. I didn't dare turn to leave because I couldn't desert Lucy in case she was still out there.

I studied the thing before me. I was amazed at how it had mimicked my pal. I looked along its body, and then I saw a tail. A long tail. It noticed me looking at its wagging appendage.

"Oh," it said, "that's right." It looked back at its own tail and grimaced. It realized that Lucy didn't have one herself. "Well, maybe we'll get it right next time." Just then, it stood up on its back legs as if it were human. It held a sharp object in its shockingly, hand-like paw. The shiny tool hit the porch light and bounced a beam into my eye. Now squinting at the object, I could see it was a cleaver. I wanted to run now, but my legs felt like they were made of concrete. I stood, frozen. The creature twisted itself around to face its own backside and took a swing at its tail, cutting it clean off. The tail, hitting the ground, turned into a two headed snake and side slithered off into the darkness. "That's better, right?" the thing asked me, returning to its original form, minus one tail. Its body now looked just like Lucy's, but the face still had an evil, almost human grin. "Now can we play?"

"Aaaaaahhh!!!" I let out a loud scream. I leapt up and found myself back in bed. I was shaking with terror. Sweat was pouring from my face, and my pajamas were soaked. It was a nightmare; but it felt so real. My eyes darted around the room to make sure I was back in touch with reality. Everything was in its appropriate place, and I was alright. I took a few deep breaths to calm down. I looked to the end of the bed, and Lucy wasn't there.

"Lucy," I whispered, scared the creature from my dream might be listening. "Lucy, where are you?" I heard a low growl from under the bed. The growl was familiar. I'd heard her growl at things before like stray cats and the mail man. I reluctantly scooted myself to the edge of the bed and leaned over to look under. I carefully lifted the bed skirt and saw Lucy hunched in the corner, growling at nothing. I took a moment to search back and forth, but I still saw nothing under there except for her. I clicked my tongue inside my cheek softly. She heard this and immediately came up from under the bed as if everything was fine. I patted the side of my bed with my left hand, and she jumped right back up, taking her usual spot.

I settled back into the covers. My pillow was wet with perspiration, but I couldn't bring myself to expose my arm and flip it over. The room was stifling with summer heat. It had to have been nearly 90 degrees in that bedroom, but I insisted on keeping the covers on. I was terrified, and the blankets, I felt, made some kind of protective shield. I rested easier knowing Lucy was with me, and I tried to tell myself it was just a dream, but a large part of me couldn't shake the idea that it might be something more.

It took a long time for me to fall back to sleep that night, but I do remember the rest of the night being completely dream free.

I didn't tell my mom or dad about the dream. In fact, I didn't talk about it with anyone. At the time, I was so afraid of the thing I met in that dream, that it seemed talking about it might make it real. I chose to ignore it and go on with my summer.

Lucy and I went on the next week or so dividing our time between the creek and the front lawn sprinklers. It was hot, almost record breaking hot, that summer. My friend Bobby came over to hang out a couple times. Whenever he was around, I could tell Lucy would get a little jealous, but we always tried to include her in whatever we were up to. Bobby and I decided one day to make a tree swing out of an old tire my dad had stored in the garage. We took some heavy rope and tied it around the tire and then scoped the yards for the best tree. The perfect tree swing tree was right in my backyard. It had thick sturdy branches and a solid foundation.

Bobby elected me the tire swing hanger. I probably should have known better. I wasn't supposed to climb these trees unsupervised, but my mom wasn't due home for another hour and my dad for even longer. I figured, *what the hell. I'm almost a teenager, and teenagers are almost adults, and almost is good enough, right?* Wrong! That was the hardest fall I'd ever taken. I broke my arm, and I was sentenced to a cast for the rest of my summer. That wasn't even the worst part. Because of my, as my parents put it, *dangerous stunt,* I was also condemned to two weeks grounding and no unsupervised play dates for the rest of break. It was a bummer to say the least, but I still had my ever faithful Lucy to play with.

The first couple weeks with that cast were nearly unlivable. I couldn't stand the heat. I wasn't allowed to leave the house since I was grounded, and I found myself insanely bored. When my parents were at work, Lucy and I amused ourselves with television. One day during that time, I was settled on the couch watching one of those court shows, when Lucy jumped up and ran toward the door barking.

"What is it, Lucy?" I quickly glanced over at the VCR and saw it was 3:01 in the afternoon. Mom would be home in an hour.

I jumped up and joined Lucy at the door. I looked out, and no one was there.

"You're silly. What are you barking at? You wanna go outside?" I opened the screen for her, and she leapt out into the front yard. I checked around the side to make sure the gate was shut and then went back to my show.

A few minutes later, I heard Lucy barking again. I went to the front door and stepped out onto the porch. The sun was almost blinding. I shielded my eyes with my right hand as I moved down the steps and met my dog on the lawn. She was now sniffing fervently. As I looked down at her, I heard something behind me. I turned quickly and saw Lucy behind me. I swiveled back to my original position and she was still there. She was in two places at the same time. I jerked backward and watched both dogs in front of me. As I stood, trying to figure out just what I was seeing, I felt something lick my hand. I pulled my hand up and stumbled a few steps backward. I looked and saw a third dog. All were identical. My head whipped around from dog to dog to dog. They were all Lucy. At least, they all looked like Lucy.

"Lucy?" I called quietly, hoping one of them would reveal themselves to be my true companion.

Simultaneously, they lifted their heads toward me.

"Lucy?" I called out again.

"Yes?" they all hissed in unison.

I toppled over backward and landed on the grass beneath me. There were three of them. Their faces began to contort as the creature's had in my dream before. *Wait*. I thought to myself. *Is this a dream?*

"Wake up!" I started yelling. "Wake up!" It didn't work. I was still there, and so were they.

They began walking in my direction. I tried to scoot along, moving my hands and feet in a crab like fashion, but they were closing in. I heard snarls from behind me, and I flipped around to see three more of them. I scrambled to get myself to my feet. I spun slowly as they circled me. Six dogs; Six Lucy clone dogs, smiling at me. Each had blood dripping from their crooked smile. Their fur was slicked down with some kind of goop.

"Stop," I said, putting my hands out, trying to use my cast as some sort of barrier, "just go away."

One of them leapt forward, mouth open. It seemed to come at me in slow motion, yet I couldn't get away from it in time. The large mouth grew bigger and bigger. Its jaw seemed disjointed as it went for my protected forearm. It latched on to my cast and started flailing its body around as it attacked me. I could hear its teeth cutting into the plaster. I felt the jerking of my bones, and tears were streaming down my face. I looked down and tried to pull the dog off using my other hand, but it was too strong. Somehow, its teeth were sharp enough to break through and were now ripping into my flesh. I screamed in pain and pleaded, and finally it let go and laughed as it watched me tumble back in pain.

"Oh relax," said the leader from the opposite side of the circle. "We're just playing." Its voice crept inside my head. I don't think I ever actually saw its lips move when it spoke. Its voice was just, there.

I looked down, and my cast was whole again. The pain had also subsided. I took in as much air as I could; I was almost unable to breathe at all.

"Come on, kid. Which one of us do you want to play with next?" It gurgled as it laughed in my direction.

"Simon!" a familiar voice called from the sky. "Simon Andrew!" I looked up to see my mother standing over me. I was back on the couch. "I told you not to watch television while I was out. Is this what you've been doing the whole time you've been grounded?"

"Uh..." I looked around to make sure none of the creatures had followed me into the house. I then realized that I had been dreaming again. I must have fallen asleep on the couch. "Oh, I'm sorry, Mom. We got bored."

"We? You had someone over?" She looked angry.

"No. Me and Lucy. We got bored."

"Okay," she conceded, "and it's Lucy and I." She never could resist correcting my grammar. "Well, I'm going to start dinner. I would like you to set the table for me, alright?"

"Alright." I got up and made my way to the front to check on Lucy. I peered out the window and saw her playing in the yard. She was just fine, but I didn't remember actually letting her out before the dream.

"Hey, Mom?"

"Yes," she replied.

"Did you let Lucy out?" I asked suspiciously.

"Yes, I did."

My imagination had gotten the best of me. Of course that dream wasn't real.

"I can't believe you slept through all that barking," my mom continued, "she wanted outside pretty badly."

I mulled that over for a few seconds, but I told myself it didn't mean anything. She could have been barking for any old reason. I set the table like my mom had requested, and I got ready for dinner.

That night, I was too scared to go to sleep. I sat on my bed and watched Lucy sleep. I did everything I could to stay awake. I did jumping jacks; I played solitaire; I even organized my closet, something my mom had been bugging me about for weeks. All my efforts were dashed in the two o'clock hour when my tired eyes had finally had enough. I convinced myself I was being ridiculous, and I put myself to bed.

An hour later, I woke to a strange tapping sound coming from the closet. I looked at the clock. Again it read *3:01*. I could feel a rush of fear induced adrenaline coarse through my body. My heart felt heavy, and my throat went dry. Lucy was standing in front of the closet door, on point.

I went over the options in my head. I could get up and find absolutely nothing; I could get up and find a mouse making a home out of one of my shoes; or I could get up and as soon as my feet touched the floor, get pulled under the bed and attacked by a vicious fanged creature. After weighing all the options, I decided the first two were the most likely. Besides, what kind of man would I be if I let a little nightmare cripple me in such a way? I figured I should just get up and let Lucy inspect the stupid closet.

Even though I'd decided there weren't any creatures under the bed, I still got up with the utmost caution. I timidly placed my feet on the carpet, trying not to make a sound. I stepped lightly, so as not to let the floor creak beneath me. My heart still felt heavy in my chest, and I held my breath as I went for the door knob. I slowly turned it and paused when I heard the springs in the knob click. I let go, gathered myself, and tried again. This time I moved quickly. I turned the knob, swung open the closet door, and jumped back, ready to fight. Lucy raced inside the closet and sniffed around, finding nothing. I realized I hadn't taken a breath yet and inhaled deeply with relief.

Lucy came back toward me a little disappointed. She really wanted it to be a mouse. Maybe it was, but it was definitely hiding by now.

"See, girl, nothing to be afraid of. Nothing there." I patted her on the head and shut the closet door behind me.

As I moved confidently back to my bed, I was stopped short when I heard a growl. My breath stopped again as I turned slowly back toward the closet door. It was muffled behind the door, but it was definitely a growl, growing louder and deeper. Lucy matched it with a growl of her own as she approached the closet.

The growl was then amplified through the room. I could hear it all around me, but whatever was making the noise was still in that closet, now digging at the door.

"Simon..." the thing said. I recognized the voice. It was the same demon, dog-like creature I'd faced before. "I'm hungry, Simon..." it called, lingering on each word, with a rattle behind each breath.

Lucy was now barking and snarling. She was ready to fight. I ran to my bedroom door. I wasn't as sure about standing up to this thing as Lucy was. Why weren't my mom and dad woken by Lucy's barking? Where were they? I tried to turn the bedroom door knob to get out, but my hands kept slipping off of it. I couldn't get a good enough grip. I wanted to call out to my parents. I opened my mouth to scream, but was cut off by the angry voice of the intruder.

"They won't hear you, Simon!" it claimed. "But don't worry, little boy; when I'm done with you, I'll visit them too."

NO! I screamed in my head. *GO AWAY!*

"I will, just as soon as we're done playing."

It responded to my thoughts. It was in my head. I looked around for any kind of weapon I could find. I had a baseball bat in the corner. I made a move for it. Just as my fingertips touched the handle, the bat flew over me and stuck to the ceiling. I was defenseless. Any plan I might come up with to fight back would be foreseen by this thing.

I threw myself to the ground and hugged my legs tight, putting my head down. I suppose I thought curling up into a ball would make it more difficult for the demon dog to rip into me. I also had this thought that if I couldn't see it, maybe it didn't exist, so I closed my eyes tight.

I heard the closet door fly open. The sound startled me, but I didn't dare look up. I knew what I would see. I stayed in position and decided to keep doing so and ride it out. It really seemed like all I could do. I heard something moving toward me, and I clutched my legs even harder, praying it would go away. Then I heard Lucy. She ran from the opposite side of the carpet and leapt onto the creature. I heard snarling and tearing. I was terrified that if I looked up I would see my friend being torn to shreds. This went on for a few moments, until I heard the whimper. It wasn't hers though. I then heard a slither across the bedroom floor, and the closet door slammed shut.

I was still afraid to look up. I felt something lick my arm. Lucy! I looked up, and there she was. She was panting, but she was in one piece.

"Lucy! Are you alright?" I checked her over, and I didn't see a single scratch on her. I looked around the room and searched for any sign of the creature, but it was gone. Then I went to the closet. Fear took over again as I closed my eyes and turned the knob.

Lucy started barking like crazy again. I let go of the door knob and opened my eyes to find I was actually lying in bed. Confused, I glanced at the clock. It was 3:02. It seemed I had just been dreaming... again, but Lucy really was barking. Something about the way she was barking told me that these dreams weren't just a result of a bad food choice before bed time. It felt real. I couldn't have imagined it.

I sat up and saw Lucy staring up at the ceiling. She resumed barking as she watched whatever she was staring at cross the ceiling, run down the wall and find its way out the window. She chased the invisible creature to the window sill. The window was cracked open, and whatever it was left. She barked after it for a few seconds, then satisfied it was gone, she quit, turned back toward me, and joined me on the bed.

I leapt from bed and closed the window. I wasn't sure what she had just chased out, but I had a feeling that as long as I didn't let it, it wouldn't be back.

I was startled as my bedroom door swung open. My dad stood in the doorway.

"What is going on in here?" he said.

"Nothing. Sorry, Dad. Lucy saw a mouse, but it scurried away. I'm not sure where it is now." I didn't want to tell him what I really saw. I wouldn't even know how to explain it. *I had a nightmare about a creepy dog, and I'm pretty sure it came to life, and Lucy chased it away* sounds a little nuts, even for a twelve year old. He'd probably tell me my imagination ran away with me and restrict me from certain movies and books.

"A mouse?" he asked. "Ah, man. Guess I have to set some traps. Okay, well... goodnight." He shut the door, and I heard the thudding of his feet as he wobbled back down the hall.

I curled up at the end of my bed with Lucy. I gave her a huge hug and thanked her for saving me. She licked my face and settled back into sleep.

The rest of that night, I slept really well. I did have a dream, but I don't really remember it. I've had a lot of dreams since, and probably a few nightmares, but none that haunted me in the same way. I can tell you this for sure, I never dreamt of that creature again, and whatever Lucy chased out of my bedroom that night, didn't dare come back.

ALL SALES ARE FINAL

The large mirror reflected the sun as Kathy set it against the back table on the lawn.

"Ah!" Mike shouted. He shielded his eyes with one arm as he walked across the grass. "Babe, you could hurt someone. Here let me," he said, chuckling to himself as he took the sizeable wall mirror and moved it under the shade of the tree.

"Thanks. Sorry, I didn't realize," Kathy apologized.

"That's okay. It looks good there, yeah?"

"Yeah, perfect." Kathy grabbed a table cloth and made her way to a side table. There were six tables on the lawn. Two folding tables they'd recovered from the basement, an end table and coffee table from the living room, a small desk from the study, and the dining room table were all arranged around the front lawn and decorated with items from inside the house. Kathy didn't like how cheap one of the folding tables appeared, and so she decided to dress it up with a lace table cloth she'd found in the linen closet. She carefully placed the antique items from the table top on the grass and unfolded the cloth over the surface.

"Hey, that looks nice," Mike said as he wrapped his arms around Kathy's waist from behind.

"Just thought I should class it up a little." Kathy smiled as she went over the creases with her hand. She wriggled out of Mike's hold and returned to the items on the grass, arranging them once more on the table.

"Well, Kath, I think this is going to be a very lucrative day. It looks good, real good."

"I hope so. She has some great stuff here. I can't believe the condition of these antiques. She must've really taken care of this stuff." Kathy crossed her arms and looked around. The Colorado sun warmed the trees and flowers, filling the air with the sweet smell of early summer. She breathed it in as she marveled at all the antiques and treasures.

"What do you think you're doing?" A rusty female voice broke Kathy's concentration.

The couple turned to see a short, elderly woman crossing the driveway. She had a stern scowl on her wrinkled face. Her little body seemed very tense under her gray sweater.

"Hello there." Mike offered a warm greeting and met her at the edge of the grass.

"Just what in the hell do you think you are doing? Who are you?" the woman demanded.

"Hi. You must be Mrs. Rosewood," Mike said as he extended his right hand, but when the gesture was not returned, he continued, "I'm Mike Porter, and this is my wife, Kathy. I'm Millie's nephew." He motioned toward the house. "My aunt has asked us to take care of some final things before the house officially goes on the market. We're just getting rid of some of the things she can't take with her and cleaning the place up before we show it."

"On the market? Millie never said anything about moving." Her tone remained unyielding and skeptical.

"Well, as you know, she's really getting on in years, and unfortunately, she's been having a lot of trouble lately. Just last night the poor thing had a fall and had to be rushed to the hospital. We've finally convinced her it's just not safe for her to live alone anymore, and so she's decided to give up the house and move home with us. We would love to keep all her things, but honestly, we just don't have the room. She agreed to the yard sale. Oh, and don't worry, she's doing alright. She just has some bruising. She should be able to come home soon."

"Well..." Mrs. Rosewood turned her head toward the ground and huffed. "I would like to see her. Maybe I'll just take a trip on over to the hospital."

"Oh gosh, you know, they have her on so many drugs right now, and she really needs her rest. How about I tell her you stopped by, and I'll have her give you a call when she's up to it?"

"Fine, fine. You let her know I came by," the woman ordered.

"Of course," Mike said sweetly. "Would you like to look around and see if there's anything of hers you might fancy?"

"No. I would not." With that Mrs. Rosewood turned back toward the driveway and crossed over onto her own lawn, making sure to look back and take one last survey of the situation before heading up the steps into her own house.

"Charming woman," Kathy said.

"Yes." Mike's gaze lingered on the house next door.

"Mike," Kathy interrupted, "let's finish this up. People should be coming soon."

"Right!" Mike snapped back to the task at hand. "You have all the flyers out? And the signs?"

"Sure do! Just help me move out the dining room chairs and that loveseat from the living room, and we'll be set."

"Not the couch?" Mike smiled wide.

"No." Kathy laughed. "Definitely not the couch. We need that."

By noon, most of the neighborhood and several people from around town had been by to check out the sale and inquire about poor Millie. She was very well known in the community, and most were very saddened by the news that she would be leaving, but it didn't stop them from rifling through and purchasing her things.

A lot of them were shocked to see Mike and Kathy heading the sale. Millie had never really talked about family; most thought she was left completely alone after her husband passed several years before. They'd never heard of her successful lawyer nephew and his beautiful wife until now. Mike explained to several of them that his dear Aunt Millie was very private when it came to family matters. Though they kept in touch and were very close, there was some feuding between Millie and Mike's mother. Talking about Mike usually triggered a long discussion about his mother, and Millie had simply learned to avoid that scenario. The bargain hunters understood and empathized with Mike and Kathy over their poor ailing aunt.

A couple hours later, the tables were beginning to look bare. The cash box was stuffed, and the pair thought it might be a good idea to go inside while there was a lull in lawn traffic and dump it out. They were excited to see just how much the sale had pulled in so far. They counted quickly, stuffed the cash into a large envelope, and headed for the front door.

A large man in a police uniform greeted them in the doorway. He removed his hat and stood on the welcome mat.

"Hello, Officer," Mike said calmly. "Come to look around the sale?"

"No, sir. I'm sorry to disturb you, but I was driving by, and I saw the tables, and I thought I'd stop in and say hello to Mrs. Porter. Is she home?"

"No, Officer, she's in the hospital. Bless her heart." Mike continued to explain how she'd had a fall the night before and was in the hospital recovering. He also explained that she would soon be joining him and Kathy at their home in Florida.

"So I take it you don't have a permit for this yard sale then? Here in Sun Ridge, we do require a permit for selling."

"Gosh, no, sir, we don't have a permit. It's just all been happening so fast. We're just trying to do the best we can to get her affairs in order before she moves. Poor thing just can't do these things for herself. I really wish we could take it all with us, but, you know, space. She said she didn't need anything but the clothes in her dresser and us. Isn't that sweet?"

"That sounds like Millie," he said as he peeked around the couple in the doorway. "Nice photo," he complimented a picture of Mike and Kathy on Millie's hallway table.

"Thank you," Kathy chimed in. "That was taken on our honeymoon."

"Alright." He exhaled nervously. "Go ahead with the yard sale, but please make sure you're packed up by five, and please don't put it all out again tomorrow. I don't want to get in trouble now."

"No problem. Thank you, Officer..." Mike examined his name tag and continued, "Marquez, Officer Marquez. We sure do appreciate it. Millie will too."

"Well, I sure hope she is alright. Please give her my regards." He placed his hat back on his head and turned toward the front steps.

"Sure will," Mike called after him.

Officer Marquez waved as he walked toward his car.

A couple hours and four sales later, Mike and Kathy decided to call it a day. The yard sale was a great success. The few items that remained were easily toted back into the house. The two had the lawn back to naked within a half hour. All that remained were outlines in the grass from where the blades had done their best to support the weight of the tables.

Inside, Kathy and Mike sat close together on the couch, basking in the success of their day. Kathy cuddled up to Mike's chest as he counted their intake.

"That's a lot of money, babe." Kathy's eyes were wide with excitement. "Where's our next stop?"

"Well," Mike said as he shuffled the bills back and forth between his fingers for the fifth time, "I was reading an article on the internet today about a widow in Maine with quite an impressive art collection. No children, lives in a quaint little town. I think we should head out to Maine for the weekend. What do you think?"

"Sounds lovely, darling," Kathy replied as she hugged him tighter.

A knock at the door interrupted their daydream.

"No, no, Aunt Millie," Mike said as he and Kathy rose from the couch. "Don't get up. We'll see who it is." The couple looked at each other and laughed as they went for the door.

Mike swung it open to find a very worried looking Mrs. Rosewood.

"I went to the hospital. Millie wasn't there. Where is she?" Her tone was even more demanding and angry than before.

"Well hello, Mrs. Rosewood. Millie's home now actually. She's still a little out of it, but I'm sure she'd love to see you. Come on in," Mike offered as he motioned down the hallway toward the living room.

Mrs. Rosewood huffed and pushed past him. She charged down the hallway and saw Millie from behind, sitting on the couch.

"Millie," Mrs. Rosewood called calmly, "Millie, dear, are you alright?"

The old woman made her way around the side of the couch and gazed down in horror as Millie's face came in to view. She was propped up on the couch; her eyes were closed, her body very still, and all color was drained from her face. Mrs. Rosewood could see a small purple line on Millie's neck coming out from the collar of her blouse. She leaned in and pulled the collar downward to reveal a long purple choke line across Mrs. Porter's throat.

"Millie!" Mrs. Rosewood cried out. She stood and put her hands to her face. Tears welled up in her eyes as she realized her friend was dead. She knew she should run, she should scream, she should do something, but she was frozen with fear.

She then felt a sharp tug from behind and a relentless pain and tightness around her own neck. She struggled to get away, but her attacker had overpowered her. She stared into Millie's lifeless face as the life left from her own. She gave one feeble kick as a last attempt to get away, but it was too late. With that, she too was gone.

"Ugh!" Kathy let out a large grunt and then took a big breath in as she released the nylon rope, letting Mrs. Rosewood fall to the floor. "You get the next one. That hurt my hands."

"Aw, sorry, babe." Mike went to Kathy's side and put his arm around her. He picked up the body and lifted it up onto the couch next to Millie. "They look so peaceful. Don't they look cute sitting here together?"

"Yeah, but where am I supposed to sit now?" Kathy asked as Mike picked up the rope and fixed the couch pillows.

"In the car," Mike laughed, nudging her gently with his elbow. "Come on. Let's get ready for our trip."

"Okay." Kathy made a pouty face. Mike kissed her, and the two went about their ritual.

The rope always went with them. A murder weapon would never be found. The two never worried much about finger prints. Neither of them had been arrested before, so their prints weren't in the database, but just to be safe, they would wipe down the things they used most, like the door knobs and the sink handles. The stuff from the yard sales wasn't of concern being that so many people touched those things during the day, it would be nearly impossible to pin down just one person.

"Kath!" Mike called out from the kitchen, "Don't forget our picture!"

"On it!" Kathy replied as she grabbed their honeymoon photo off the hallway table. They liked to put it out in every house they visited. It made them feel more at home wherever they were; plus it helped when the occasional snoopy neighbor or cop happened by.

"Alright." Kathy looked around, making sure they hadn't forgotten anything. "I think that's it."

Mike joined her by the door.

"Let's skedaddle, Kath."

"I'm sick of Mike and Kathy. This next one, let's be John and Lindsay from Chicago again. They're fun!"

"You got it, Linds." Mike kissed her sweetly as they walked out, closing the door and wiping the handle behind them.

They made their way to the street, where their Mercedes was parked. The car was a gift from one of their dear aunts. The plates would be changed of course once they hit the next state. It was a minor inconvenience worth suffering to drive such a beautiful car. Off they went with a map and a dream.

"What's the weather like this time of year in Maine?" Lindsay asked.

"It's beautiful, baby," John answered. "Perfect weather for a yard sale."

ABOUT THE AUTHOR

Elizabeth Fields grew up in the small town of Los Alamos, California. Dreaming of the big city and bright lights, Elizabeth moved to Los Angeles at the age of 20 and found success as an actress and model. She has been working steadily in the entertainment industry, appearing on television and in film and magazines. At a very young age, Elizabeth found herself drawn to the written word. She is an avid reader and has enjoyed writing since childhood. She is known by her family and friends for her creative flare, and she has always said that there is nothing more exciting than putting your imagination to work. For more information on Elizabeth, please visit elizabethfields.net.

NOTE FROM THE AUTHOR

Thank you for reading *Don't Let Them In*. I hope you enjoyed reading the stories as much as I liked writing them. I am a huge fan of anything and everything horror, and I hope to be bringing you more scary tales soon. For more information about me and my other work, or if you'd like to contact me, please visit elizabethfields.net.